Blinded by the muzzle blast
of the shot fired from the door...

Jessie triggered off an unaimed shot from her Colt.
She heard the slug crash through the door with a
splintering of hard wood.

Beside her, Ki slid a *shuriken* blade from his wrist-
case into his hand, and stepped out of the line of fire
from inside the house. He stood poised, ready to
launch the razor-edged throwing blade at anyone who
came through the dark doorway...

WESLEY ELLIS

LONE STAR

AND THE OUTLAW POSSE

JOVE BOOKS, NEW YORK

LONE STAR AND THE OUTLAW POSSE

A Jove Book / published by arrangement with
the author

PRINTING HISTORY
Jove edition / August 1987

ISBN: 0-515-09114-6

Jove Books are published by The Berkley Publishing Group,
200 Madison Avenue, New York, New York 10016.
The name "JOVE" and the "J" logo
are trademarks belonging to Jove Publications, Inc.

PRINTED IN THE UNITED STATES OF AMERICA

10 9 8 7 6 5 4 3 2 1

Chapter 1

A hint of daylight creeping under the drawn window shades was enough to waken Jessie Starbuck, accustomed as she was to getting up at the first signs of dawn. She did not stir when her eyes first opened, but lay staring up at the ceiling. After a moment she realized that it did not have the familiar border design of her room at the Circle Star. She lay motionless, staring at the ceiling with its ornate fresco, missing the familiar sounds of the big Texas ranch. Still only half awake, Jessie listened for the noises that she was missing.

She was used to awakening to the sound of an occasional whinny of a horse in one of the corrals, mingled with the faint clatter of pots and pans from the cookshack and the grating of high-heeled boots on hard-baked, arid soil as the ranch hands went from the bunkhouse to breakfast.

Then a cool breath from the window, the fog-moistened air of San Francisco, reminded her where she was. She got

1

a second reminder a few seconds later when the man lying beside her stirred in his sleep. Then memories of the night came flooding back to her.

Shifting her head a bit on the pillow, Jessie looked at her bed partner. He was still asleep, stretched out on his back. She could see only his rugged profile, outlined in the light that steadily grew brighter around the edges of the window shades. As her eyes became accustomed to the dimness, Jessie studied him, looking at his high brow under a tousel of black hair, his straight nose, his full moustache that almost hid his curving, sensual lips, his jutting chin that even in the dim dawn light showed a hint of dark stubble.

As though Jessie's lingering scrutiny had reached through his sleep, the man stirred and then turned toward her. His eyes opened and he smiled.

"Good morning, dear Jessie," he said softly.

"Good morning, Hal," she replied. "I hope I didn't wake you up, but I'm in the habit of getting out of bed early at the Circle Star."

"I usually wake up about now when I'm at home," Hal Parnam replied. "But I don't have a lovely lady like you with me. And I don't intend to let you get away, either."

"Suppose I run before you catch me," Jessie smiled.

She made a move as though to leave the bed, but Hal's hand caught her wrist and pulled her to him. Jessie did not resist; vivid memories of the night just ending were already beginning to arouse her. She let Parnam pull her close, and when he lowered his head to seek her lips she turned to meet him. The bristle of his moustache brushed across her face, and then his mouth was glued to her, his tongue-tip running questingly along her lips.

Jessie yielded to Parnam's kiss and met his tongue with hers. The weight of his chest was on her now. The warmth of his body and the gentle rasping of the curls that covered his chest were having an effect on Jessie. She felt the tips of her full breasts starting to bud and twisted her shoulders a bit, rubbing her trim body against his to enhance the

2

sensations that were beginning to surge through her.

After a few moments, as her excitement continued to mount, Jessie brushed her free hand down her lover's side to his flanks and closed around the cylinder of flesh that was already firm and burgeoning. With an almost inaudible sigh of anticipation she guided Parnam and clasped his hips between her thighs as he sank into her.

Time stood still for a long while now, the silence of the room broken only by the sighs of the lovers as their embrace was prolonged to the peak of ecstasy. Finally the peak was reached and passed, and Jessie's cries of pleasure faded. They turned to lie side by side in relaxed silence.

After the minutes had ticked away, Hal sought Jessie's lips again, and, as they broke their kiss, he whispered, "I'm not going to leave you yet, Jessie. It's much too soon for us to part."

"I'm not any more anxious to see you leave than you are to go," she replied.

Twisting in his arms, Jessie pushed her lover's shoulders to the mattress until he shifted to lie on his back. Their fleshly connection had not been broken while they were resting, and for several minutes Jessie contented herself with kisses and small movements of her hips. Then she felt Hal beginning to swell within her, and she gradually increased the vigor of her motion until she was swaying with the tempo of a triphammer.

Hal's hands sought her breasts and she leaned forward until he could reach them with his lips. The added sensation of his caresses stimulated Jessie to greater efforts. She moved faster and pressed herself to him with increased force until the mounting waves of sensation swept over her faster and faster.

Hal's eyes were closed now, and she could tell from his stertorous gasps that he was as ready as she was. She speeded up with a final frenzied twisting of her hips as she rocked to and fro until Hal gasped and quivered. Then she let her own needs take control and sped to the climax that again left both of them gasping and spent.

Once more they lay quietly as the ecstasy they'd shared died away in fading ripples. A quarter hour or more passed before either of them spoke. It was Parnam who broke the spell of silence that had gripped them.

"You were very sure last night that I couldn't persuade you to give up living on that ranch in Texas and stay here as my wife," he said. "Are you just as sure this morning?"

"You know my reasons, Hal," Jessie replied. "The Circle Star was Alex's legacy to me, along with all the other things he created before he was killed."

"But that was several years ago," he objected. "Jessie, you can't live in the past, or bring Alex back."

"I know I can't bring Alex back, but I don't intend to forget him, either," she said soberly. "Could you forget your parents, Hal?"

"Of course I couldn't!"

"Then why do you expect me to push all my memories of Alex aside? I'm not any different from you in remembering the past."

"That's not exactly what I meant, Jessie. It's because I want my parents to be remembered that I want to marry and have children who'll carry on my family's name."

Jessie shook her head. "It isn't the same thing, Hal. Your children would carry on your father's name. Mine wouldn't be called Starbuck."

Frowning, Parnam said, "I've never heard of such a thing being done, but if that's what's keeping you from saying 'yes' to my proposal to marry you, we could give Starbuck to our son as his middle name."

In spite of the serious tone their discussion had taken on, Jessie smiled. "I suppose we could, Hal. *If* I changed my mind about marrying you, and *if* we had a son, and *if* your parents didn't object."

"You're raising a lot of improbable barriers," Parnam objected.

"I'm just being practical," she replied soberly. "But let's

4

not end a wonderful night in a quarrel, Hal. Even though the men who murdered Alex have paid for their crimes, I can't turn my back on what he left me. You should be able to understand that."

"I suppose I do," Parnam told her. "If you put it that way, I'm carrying on the same kind of life my father led. He didn't press me or try to persuade me to choose banking as my career, but he certainly made it easy for me to follow in his footsteps."

"That's the point I was trying to make," Jessie nodded.

"But I still want you to marry me, Jessie," Parnam went on. "I know I'll never find another woman as lovely and as fascinating as you are."

"That's a very sweet compliment," she said. "But I don't think marriage is for me. Don't let's disagree, Hal. We can still see one another when you pass through Texas on your way east, and when I come out here to San Francisco."

"I suppose I'll have to settle for that," he said after a moment. "But it doesn't mean I'll stop asking. And I suppose you're going to be too busy today for us to see one another before you leave."

"I'm afraid so," Jessie nodded. "I've got a lot of loose ends to tie up before Ki and I leave. He was planning to stay in Chinatown last night, but as soon as he gets back we'll be busy until train-time. I'm anxious to get back to Texas and the Circle Star before the hands start the gather."

"I'm not a rancher," Parnam said, and frowned. "But my guess is that what you're talking about is something like a roundup?"

"On a small scale," Jessie nodded. "The hands cut out the cattle that are ready to go to market, and put them in a separate herd."

Parnam had been dressing while they talked, but Jessie had stayed in bed, a sheet pulled up to shield her from the cool San Francisco breeze that wafted in through the open window. He bent over Jessie for a farewell kiss, stood at

5

the door for a moment looking at her, then sighed and shook his head.

"I always hate to leave you, Jessie," he said. "But I can't come up with any reason to stay, except to tell you that I'd like for you to."

"And I hate to see you go," she replied. "But I know you have your own business matters to attend to. Goodbye until the next time, Hal."

"Make it soon, will you?"

"As soon as I can," Jessie replied. "And I'll send you a telegram when I leave, just as I always do."

"I'll be waiting for you, then."

After Hal Parnam had gone, closing the door behind him, Jessie lay quietly thoughtful. The discussion she'd just finished had reminded her strongly of Alex, and she did not even try to banish memories from her mind as she lay in the quietness of the room in the Palace Hotel, staring in the gathering light at its fancifully ornamented ceiling.

Alex Starbuck had created the vast Circle Star Ranch in Southwest Texas, which Jessie looked upon as home. The ranch had been the place to which Alex had retreated after Jessie's mother died giving birth to their only child. Covering more area than many small European countries, the Circle Star was home to Jessie as it had been to her father. To the outside world, however, the ranch was only one link in the vast chain of business and industrial properties she'd inherited after Alex's death.

After her father's murder by the vicious European cartel, which Jessie and Ki had finally shattered and obliterated, Jessie had been away from the ranch for over a year, and not only to avoid sad memories. That much time had been required for her to learn the details of the financial empire that had been her inheritance.

With Ki as her faithful companion, Jessie had visited the Starbuck mines in California, Nevada, Arizona, and Montana. Through the prominent San Francisco attorney who managed Alex's legal affairs, she'd learned of the Oriental export firm that had been Alex's first business venture, which had grown into a complex of steel mills, shipyards, timber stands, and vast tracts of prime agricultural land in California's Central Valley as well as in the western fringe of the Midwestern states.

There'd been details to learn, of banks along the West Coast, brokerage houses, and more banks in the financial centers, New York and Chicago. Because no man with Alex's vast holdings could turn his back on national politics, there had been trips to Washington, where she'd been greeted with respect by an assortment of political figures ranging from bureau heads and military commanders all the way to the nation's commander-in-chief in the White House.

Even through the time when Jessie was struggling to master all the details of her inheritance, she'd been forced to fight the masters of the sinister European cartel that Alex had refused to join. The cartel's objective was to take over the financial and mercantile fabric of the United States and divert its resources to reviving a faltering Europe. Jessie had picked up the battle after the cartel's minions had assassinated Alex, and there had been many vicious attacks on her until at last the merciless group had been shattered.

No matter where the battle had taken her during that period, Ki had been at Jessie's side, tied by the same invisible bonds of loyalty he'd given Alex. Their relationship, formed after Alex's death, was almost that of brother and sister, though Ki showed Jessie the same respect he'd accorded Alex.

Ki, the son of a Japanese father and an American mother, had been banished by his father's tradition-bound family. He'd roamed the Orient as a soldier of fortune, perfecting the skills in the martial arts he'd learned from the master Hirata.

At last, during one of Alex's trading trips to the Far East, Ki had found a haven with Alex, who had been his father's friend. After staying at Alex's side until death parted them, Ki had transferred his loyalty to Jessie. He'd been at her side during the vicious attacks by the cartel, until together they had smashed the sinister alliance of Oriental thuggery and European high finance, and its repeated attempts to take over the vast resources of America.

Now, in the quiet of her room in the Palace Hotel, Jessie pushed aside the sad memories and concentrated on thinking about the happy prospect of returning to the Circle Star. She'd finished bathing and dressing and was ready for breakfast when a light tapping at the door told her that Ki had returned from his overnight visit to Oriental friends in San Francisco's Chinatown.

"Come in, Ki," Jessie called. "The door's not locked."

"I was afraid I'd wake you up," Ki said as he entered and closed the door behind him.

"I've been awake for quite a while," she told him. "But I haven't been hungry enough to think about breakfast."

"I had tea and rice cakes with the Nagata family," Ki said. "But that was two or three hours ago. Their oldest son wanted me to show him all the variations of the *tegatana-uke*, and it took quite a while to go through them, so I'm ready for a real breakfast now."

"And after your exercise, I'm sure you'll want to bathe and change," Jessie said. "But I'm not in any hurry. Go ahead. We can meet in the restaurant downstairs, or you can tap on my door when you're ready."

"I stopped at my room to clean up before I knocked," Ki told her. "If you're ready, we can go down to breakfast now."

As they were riding down to the main floor in one of the hotel's famous oversized elevators, Jessie remarked idly, "You know, this elevator's almost big enough for a cowhand to rope a steer in, Ki. I can't for the life of me understand why Senator Sharon had them put in."

"You know what Alex always said about the Senator and Mr. Ralston," Ki replied. "They weren't satisfied to start small and let it grow. Instead of making a modest start of one of their mining ventures, they both wanted to do things on a huge scale to begin with."

"Well, they certainly succeeded in starting big with the Palace." Jessie smiled. "I can almost swim in those big bathtubs they have here."

"I'll agree that it gives you a feeling of luxury," Ki went on. "But I'm not really comfortable in big places. In Japan, we don't have room to build on such a large scale. Why, my room at the Circle Star is big enough to hold three rooms of the house where I grew up."

They stepped out of the elevator on the main floor and started along the curving passageway that led around the inner perimeter of the hotel's famous Palm Court, which also served as a circular coach station.

At that late hour of the morning, the hotel's early risers had already left to attend to the day's business, and the late risers were still in their rooms. The wide corridor was almost deserted, and there were only two hansom cabs in the coach station. They passed a group of a half-dozen men in business suits, engaged in a debate of some sort. Jessie was surprised when one of the men lifted his hat and nodded to her. After the group had passed she turned to Ki with a puzzled frown.

"Did you recognize that man who raised his hat to me, Ki?" she asked.

Ki shook his head. "I'm sure I've seen him somewhere, but I can't remember where. And I can't recall his name, either."

"As far as I could tell, I've never seen him before," Jessie went on. "But it's probably someone from one of the banks or an office where we have some business connection."

Reaching the dining room, they were escorted by the head waiter to a linen-draped table in a secluded corner.

"Will you and your companion be having your usual breakfast fare, Miss Starbuck?" the man asked.

Jessie and Ki exchanged glances, then Jessie nodded

and replied, "That will be just fine."

Within moments a waiter arrived carrying a tray on which rested a bone china tea service. He placed the settings in front of Jessie and Ki with silent efficiency, put down a small tray on which stood a steaming teapot and a silver pot of hot water. Then he bowed and withdrew.

"We'll have to let the tea steep a few minutes," Jessie said. "It seems to be the only process that this hotel can't control."

"And from what I've heard of Senator Sharon, he's got somebody at work trying to control it right now," Ki said, and smiled.

Jessie reached for the teapot and lifted it, swirling it to circulate the boiling hot water that was still sending a wisp of steam from the spout. She was reaching across to fill Ki's cup when the head waiter returned. He carried a small silver salver in one hand.

"Pardon me for interrupting your breakfast, Miss Starbuck," the man said. He held out the silver tray. "But this gentleman has asked me to deliver his card to you and to request your permission for him to join you for a few moments."

Jessie picked up the card, glanced at it, and handed it to Ki. He read the name and title inscribed on it and looked across the table at Jessie, his eyebrows raised inquiringly.

"That's the man we passed on the way in here," Jessie said. "The one we couldn't recognize. Congressional Delegate Dawson, from Idaho. I suppose we'd better see what he wants. It must be important, or he wouldn't be here now." Turning to the head waiter she said, "Please tell the gentleman to join us."

Chapter 2

"I'm sorry to interrupt your breakfast, Miss Starbuck," Dawson began as soon as he and Jessie had exchanged greetings. "But when I passed you in the corridor I realized that you might be just the one I need to talk to."

"Perhaps you'd better sit down, then. If you haven't had breakfast yet—"

"Excuse me for interrupting, Miss Starbuck, but I've eaten my breakfast. Please don't let me interfere with yours, though."

"You're sure you wouldn't like something? Perhaps some coffee? Ki and I can't finish the pot they've brought us in addition to the tea we ordered."

"That would be fine, while we're talking."

"Of course," Jessie nodded. She signalled the waiter, who had followed Dawson to the table, and he hurried to bring another cup and saucer. As she filled the cup, Jessie went on, "I'm sure you remember Ki. He was my father's strong right hand for many years, just as he's mine now."

11

"Ki." Dawson nodded, extending his hand. "Certainly I remember you, even though it's been a long time since we met in Mr. Starbuck's office."

"Oh, I recall our meeting quite well," Ki said as he and Dawson clasped hands briefly. "It was right after Idaho Territory had failed the second time to persuade Congress to take it into the Union as a state."

"Yes," Dawson agreed. "And we're still just a Territory. We haven't stopped trying, though. I'm sure our next effort will be successful."

"I suppose that's what you came back to talk to me about?" Jessie asked.

"Exactly," Dawson nodded. "We need all the support we can muster for our next try at statehood."

"What reason did the Congress have for refusing to accept Idaho as a state?" Jessie asked.

"Pretty much the same excuse as before," Dawson replied. "Too much land and too few settlers."

"There hasn't been much migration into the area, then?" Jessie asked.

Dawson shook his head. "Very little. I'd looked for more people to settle along the Northern Pacific tracks when they were built east from Spokane a few years ago, but it just didn't happen that way."

"Perhaps that's a bit too far north to attract farmers or ranchers," Jessie suggested.

"Oh, I'll agree to that," Dawson replied. "But things have changed now. Some prospectors have just found a big new silver lode somewhere south of the Priest River, and that may bring on the population boom we need to get the Congress to vote in favor of statehood the next time we try for it."

A thoughtful frown had been growing on Jessie's face while Dawson talked. Now she said, "If I remember correctly, Alex once bought a great deal of land in the northern part of Idaho Territory."

12

"That's right," Dawson agreed. "It was in the Coeur d'Alene area, though. But that's another reason why I felt the need to talk with you."

"As I said a moment ago, I'm very glad to visit with you, but I don't see how I can be helpful," Jessie told him. "Unless it's a matter of money to help finance your next election campaign . . ."

"Well, anyone who runs for public office always welcomes a campaign contribution." Dawson smiled. "But I still have almost a year to worry about facing the voters again. And they've been very kind to me. I've had no trouble keeping my seat so far, but a year can change things pretty drastically."

"Let me know when the time comes, then," Jessie said. "I always follow my father's example in supporting the men he's found worthy of holding public office."

"That's very kind of you, Miss Starbuck." Dawson nodded. "And I'll certainly remember your offer. But it's not elections that I have on my mind right now. It's a situation that's come up with the land your father bought up in the northern part of Idaho Territory, the area they call their Panhandle. I suppose you're familiar with it?"

"Not as well as I might be," Jessie answered. "Even though I inherited Alex's land holdings, I've never even been to Idaho. I've passed through parts of it on train trips, but I'm afraid that doesn't qualify me as a resident."

"I understand that, of course." Dawson nodded. He hesitated for a moment. Then, his voice suddenly sober, he added, "Perhaps you might like to know what's happening to that land you own up in the Idaho Panhandle, Miss Starbuck."

"Of course I would," Jessie replied quickly. "From the tone of your voice, I assume it's something unpleasant."

"You'd be better qualified to judge that than I am," Dawson told her. "But having known your father, I'm sure that he'd be upset if he knew that any of his property—

13

your property now, of course, Miss Starbuck—is in danger of being used by outlaws and bandits to help them evade the law."

"That's something I find very hard to believe," Jessie said quickly. "But I'd be very interested in hearing more about it. Go ahead, Mr. Dawson."

Dawson was silent for a moment, frowning thoughtfully. At last he began, "I suppose you're familiar with the geography of Idaho Territory?"

"I know the land we're talking about now is up in the Idaho Panhandle," Jessie replied, "although I'm sure that Ki is more familiar with it than I am." Turning to Ki, she went on. "You were with Alex when he bought the property we're talking about, weren't you?"

Ki nodded. "Yes. And I remember what a long trip it was from Boise when Alex and I went there. I also remember that it was a total wilderness. No signs of settlement anywhere."

"That's right," Dawson agreed. "It was a wilderness until the latest silver discovery north of Lake Pend Oreille."

"But as I remember geography, that's almost in Canada!" Jessie exclaimed.

"Exactly," Dawson replied. "And even though the silver started south of Coeur d'Alene, it's bringing people up to the northern Idaho Panhandle. That part of the state is still pretty much of a no-man's-land, though. Once you get north of Coeur d'Alene, you're in almost completely unsettled country."

"Yes, I'm aware of that," Jessie nodded. "That's one reason I've given so little attention to the land I own up there. There's been no indication that anyone s interested in settling up there."

"You'll find that situation's changing rapidly," Dawson said quickly. "But I'm afraid it's attracting the wrong kind of settlers."

14

"Outlaws?" Jessie frowned. "Men on the run from the law?"

Dawson nodded. "Some of them. Of course, I'm aware that some sizeable parts of the western states were originally settled by men who were what they called 'on the dodge.' And quite a number of them became very good citizens."

"Is there any reason to believe that history won't repeat itself?" Jessie asked. Her voice thoughtful, she went on. "I'm not too sure that letting outlaws settle in some out-of-the-way place until they get tamed by nature is such a bad idea."

"I'm not going to comment on that, Miss Starbuck." Dawson smiled. "And to get back to the subject, my concern isn't for outlaws. It's for the good people who come into unsettled places and start building homes and establishing towns."

"Isn't that what you've just suggested is happening in the Idaho Panhandle?" she asked.

"Yes, but I'm looking at all sides of the matter. And I'm sure you must look at things much the same way. Now, tell me, would you want your land to be in the center of an outlaw's hangout and hideaway?"

"Is that what's happening on the Starbuck land?" she asked, a frown forming on her face.

"In one instance, I'm afraid it is. There's a new town being organized up on the border between the United States and Canada. As far as I've been able to determine, it's on the land your father bought years ago."

"Which means that I own it today," Jessie said thoughtfully. "Does this town have a name yet?"

"I'm not really sure," Dawson answered. "The information I have so far is very, very sketchy. I'd intended to go up there myself and investigate, but I received a telegram last evening calling me back to Washington."

"I'm beginning to understand now why you were so

15

anxious to talk to me," Jessie smiled.

Dawson returned her smile as he said, "Your mind works much like your father's did, Miss Starbuck. You have the same ability to cut right to the heart of a matter without sparring."

"If I have, I learned it or inherited it from Alex. But go on and tell me about what's happening in northern Idaho."

"I'm afraid it's in danger of becoming an outlaw's haven," the congressman said, his voice sober. "The Idaho Panhandle's not very large, you know. It's only about fifty miles across at the point where it ends at the Canadian border."

"And still very wild, I'm sure," Ki observed. "When I went with Alex to inspect the land he'd bought up there, the only way to travel was on horseback, and the only trail was the one blazed by the Lewis and Clark expedition back in the very early 1800s."

"It's changed very little since then, Ki," Dawson nodded. "When Jay Gould announced that he was going to build an east-west railroad across the northern tier of states, I did my best to persuade him to lay the tracks as close to the Canadian border as possible, but his surveyors couldn't—or maybe they just wouldn't—recommend a route that crossed all those rugged mountains between Chicago and the coast."

"There's no railroad into that part of the Territory, then?" Jessie asked.

"There is now, thanks to the feud between Jay Gould and Jim Hill. The route it takes is further south of the Canadian border than I'd like to've seen it, but from the railroad at Coeur d'Alene it's not a bad trip the rest of the way."

"If the northern part of the Idaho Panhandle is going to stay isolated, and isn't going to be a mining center, why would anybody want to build a new town up there?" Jessie asked.

"I put that question to myself when I heard about all the

activity that was reported to me," the congressman replied. "But that was before the silver lodes were discovered up there."

"They changed everything, I'm sure," she nodded.

"You're right, Miss Starbuck," he replied. "Silver makes the difference. But the richest ores have been discovered near Coeur d'Alene, and it's south of the Canadian border by almost a hundred miles."

"Then when you heard about this new town further north, out of the silver belt, you decided there wasn't any real reason for someone to build it?" Ki asked as Dawson paused longer than seemed necessary.

"Yes. And the only other answer I could think of was that some sort of illegal activity must be at the root of it."

"You mentioned an outlaw hideout a few minutes ago," Jessie said thoughtfully. "Was that your answer?"

"I'm afraid so, Miss Starbuck," Dawson nodded. "For a while I thought it might be smuggling goods back and forth between the U.S. and Canada, but with our open border secrecy's hardly necessary for smugglers. I'm convinced that the town's more likely to be what you just suggested: an outlaw hideout."

"Like Robber's Roost, or the Hole in the Wall over in Wyoming Territory?" Jessie asked.

"Not exactly," the Congressman frowned. "From what I've heard, those are hiding-places. I think this would be more of an open refuge."

"Are you suggesting a town run by outlaws?" Jessie asked.

"Something like that," Dawson agreed.

Jessie sat silent for a moment. Then she asked, "Tell me, Mr. Dawson, why are you so concerned about this new town?"

Instead of making a direct reply, Dawson countered with a question of his own. "Are you familiar with Congressional procedures, Miss Starbuck?"

"Reasonably well, I think. Why?"

"I had in mind my own situation, being just a congressional delegate rather than a full-fledged member of the House of Representatives."

"Is there a difference, then? Aren't you a congressman like all the other members?"

"Not exactly. I'm in the unfortunate position of holding the title without any of the privileges."

"Perhaps you'd better explain," Jessie suggested.

After a moment of thought, Dawson said, "I'm not suggesting that our legislative houses in Washington aren't wonderful bodies, Miss Starbuck. Unfortunately, in spite of the ringing words in our Declaration of Independence, in Congress all members are not created equal, or endowed with inalienable rights."

"That's even more cryptic than what you suggested a moment ago," Jessie smiled.

"Please don't misunderstand me," Dawson went on. "I'm very proud that the citizens of the Idaho Territory saw fit to elect me to Congress in the beginning, and that they've returned me to that office quite regularly. But if you'll look closely at the card I sent in a few minutes ago when I asked to visit with you, you'll see it doesn't say I'm a full-fledged member of the House of Representatives."

Dawson's calling-card was still lying on the table where Jessie had placed it. She glanced at it, then repeated, "Congressional delegate." Looking up at him, she asked, "Aren't you entitled to call yourself a congressman, then?"

"No, indeed. There may not seem to be any difference between a delegate and a congressman, but there certainly is."

"I suppose you had better explain, then."

"For one thing," Dawson began, "I can't originate any laws myself, and propose them to my colleagues in the House. Only congressmen are allowed to do that."

"Suppose that you need to propose a law that's badly needed by the people of Idaho Territory?" she asked. "What can you do about it?"

"Practically nothing, in a direct way. I've got to find a colleague from one of the States who'll introduce the law on my behalf."

"I don't recall that as being part of our Constitution," Jessie frowned.

"It isn't. It's in the rules the House adopted during the sessions that became very bitter just before the War Between the States erupted. Actually, its purpose was to get control of Territorial legislatures and the delegates from slave-holding states. At that time there were quite a few members who came from slave-holding areas that hadn't yet been admitted to Statehood, and the northern congressmen wanted to keep them quiet."

"But that was more than twenty years ago!" Jessie protested. "That law or rule or whatever you call it is completely out of date!"

"I agree with you, of course." Dawson nodded. "And twenty years ago there were quite a few more congressional delegates than there are today, because a number of territories were admitted to the Union just before and soon after the war."

"Why haven't the House rules been changed, then?"

"Are you familiar with the Hole Bible, Miss Starbuck?"

"I'm not a Biblical scholar, if that's what you mean, but I'm reasonably familiar with the Scriptures. Why do you ask?"

"Because when I look at the manner in which Congress does its work I'm often tempted to add a fifth item to the four wonders mentioned by the Psalmist in the thirtieth chapter."

"I'm afraid I don't recall the passage," Jessie said, shaking her head.

Dawson smiled as he replied, "The Psalmist wrote of four things which surpass all understanding. They were the way of the eagle in the air, the way of the serpent upon a rock, the way of a ship at sea and the way of a man with a maid. I'd add a fifth thing to them, the way in which the

19

Congress of the United States conducts its business."

Jessie smiled. Then the smile faded as she asked, "The House clings to old rules and customs, then?"

"Miss Starbuck, one of the few things I'm positive about is that the United States House of Representatives—and I might add, the Senate as well—never changes any of its rules, even when they're obsolete. Do you realize that the House of Representatives still has veto power over the actions of a Territorial legislature?"

"But a moment ago, you said you've found a way to get permission to speak, even if you're just a delegate instead of a full-fledged congressman," Jessie said. "Surely you've suggested that the Congress should refuse to allow this new town to be built."

"So far, I haven't found a single congressman who'll cooperate with me in getting the floor to speak, or one who's willing to introduce legislation that might stop a bunch of outlaws from building a town for themselves in any of the few Territories that remain."

"But that's incredible!" Jessie protested.

"Incredible, yes," Dawson nodded. "But a fact."

"I think I can see what you're leading up to, Mr. Dawson," Jessie said slowly. "Since I happen to own the land on which this new town's being built, you want me to stop its construction."

"I think you're the only one who can stop it. The land is yours, and since you didn't know about what's happening to it, I think I'm safe in I'm assuming you haven't sold it to them."

"I haven't sold a square inch of land in the Idaho Territory to anyone," Jessie told him. "And nobody's asked to buy any."

"Then you shouldn't have any trouble evicting these men," Dawson said quickly.

"That might not be as easy as you seem to think," she told him, frowning thoughtfully. "It'd be impossible for me to say how much trouble would be involved, if they're the

20

kind of outlaws you say they are."

"You can safely take my word that they are, Miss Star-buck." Dawson assured her.

"Oh, I don't doubt you. But in an isolated place like that the only law that's respected has to be backed up by force."

"I can be of some help in that respect," Dawson suggested. "There's a volunteer group in Lewiston that calls itself the Idaho Territorial Guard. I'm sure that I can get a few of them to go with you."

Jessie sat silently for a moment or two, her expression thoughtful, as she weighed the Congressman's request. Once she glanced at Ki, a question in her eyes. He shrugged almost imperceptibly, to indicate that he had no suggestions to offer.

Finally Jessie said, "Ki and I had planned to leave today, Mr. Dawson. We were going back to the Circle Star. How long do you think it would take for us to clear up the situation in Idaho?"

"My guess would be three weeks," Dawson replied. "A month, at most. Just getting to the Idaho Panhandle will take a week or more."

Again Jessie looked at Ki. This time she said, "I don't suppose three weeks will make a great deal of difference to the men at the Circle Star."

"It shouldn't matter a bit," Ki replied. "They'll handle the gather just like they always do, whether we're there or up in the wilds of Idaho."

"I know they will, but I just enjoy being there when they're working the cattle," Jessie replied.

"If Congressman Dawson's estimate is right, we'll still get back to the Circle Star before the market herd goes out," Ki said.

Nodding, Jessie turned to Dawson and said, "This Idaho Territorial Guard you mentioned. Could you have three or four of its members join us? Preferably some who're familiar with the area."

"I'm sure I can," Dawson nodded. "There are always a

few members of the Guard who have time to spare. Suppose I have them meet you in Coeur d'Alene? It's not yet such a big town that they'd have trouble locating you there."

"It's as good an arrangement as any," Jessie agreed. "All right, Mr. Dawson. You're correct in thinking I'd be interested in what's happening to any Starbuck property, no matter where it happens to be. I owe that to Alex's memory. Ki and I will leave for Idaho late today."

Chapter 3

"You know, Ki, I wouldn't mind this terrible trail if only I was riding Sun," Jessie said as her horse hunkered back on its hind legs and skidded down the steep slope to which the almost invisible trail had led them. "This livery horse has a terribly hard mouth."

"On steep grades like this one, I suppose we could walk and lead the horses," Ki replied. His speech was broken and jerky, for in addition to handling the reins of his own horse he was leading the pack horse, which carried their supplies.

Jessie shook her head. "I'm afraid they'd plunge downhill faster than we could walk and we'd either lose them or wind up being dragged if we'd knotted the reins. But the trail itself isn't my main worry. I'm still wondering what happened to those men from Lewiston that Congressman Dawson promised would meet us in Coeur d'Alene."

"Probably we'll never know anything more about them than the congressman told us in his telegram," Ki replied.

23

Jessie nodded, but said nothing. They rode on in silence, in the way of two who have been good companions for a long while and need no words to communicate.

True to Jessie's promise to Congressman Dawson, she and Ki had exchanged their Southern Pacific train tickets from San Francisco to Texas for passage to Spokane. There they'd switched to the Burlington Northern for the final leg of their journey to Coeur d'Alene, high in the Idaho Panhandle. Instead of being greeted there by the group of men from the Idaho Territorial Guard promised by Dawson there'd been an apologetic telegram from the congressional delegate:

TERRITORIAL GUARD MEMBERS I HAD DEPENDED ON TO GO WITH YOU NOW SAY UNABLE TO LEAVE WHEAT HARVEST STOP PLEASE ACCEPT SINCERE APOLOGIES FOR UNINTENTIONALLY MISLEADING YOU STOP HOPE IT POSSIBLE FOR YOU COMPLETE MISSION DISCUSSED

"What do we do now?" Ki had asked. "Change our plans again and go back to the Circle Star?"

For a moment Jessie had not replied. Then she'd said slowly and thoughtfully, "No, I don't think so, Ki. Since we've come this far already, it'd be a shameful waste to turn around and go home without even looking at the land Alex bought up here all those years ago."

"Somehow, I had an idea that's what you might say." Ki smiled. "You're as stubborn as Alex about finishing a job you've decided to take on."

"Perhaps it's just as well that Dawson's men couldn't join us," Jessie had gone on thoughtfully. "We've handled things like this by ourselves before. If we had somebody else with us, they might just get in our way."

"But I can't recall a time when we faced the prospect of having an entire town against us," Ki reminded her.

"There've been a few occasions when it's seemed a whole town was on the other side, though." She smiled.

"So there have," Ki agreed.

"And since we've decided to go on, I don't see any reason for wasting time." Jessie had continued. "This town's big enough to have a good livery stable or two where we can hire horses, and enough stores where we can buy almost anything we need. It's still early enough to get a trail outfit together. We'll spend the rest of the day here and get an early start in the morning."

Now, nearing the close of their second day out of Coeur d'Alene, they were travelling over the least broken land they'd yet encountered. In spite of its pronounced upward slant, the trail was smoother than any of the terrain they'd encountered since turning off the rough wagon road that ran parallel to the railroad tracks, and taking the narrow beaten trail that led almost due north.

It was a rugged land through which the trail was taking them. Pines whose tips seemed to touch the cloudless blue sky grew thickly, the faintly marked path meandering between them. Now and then the trail veered to one side or the other, to avoid a steep slope or a short dropoff, in the fashion of trails that had originally been beaten by the heavily laden pack animals of trappers and prospectors.

Such a trail as they were following was seldom straight, for both the men and the animals who travelled over it almost always carried heavy loads. Jessie and Ki were no exception. They'd also found it easier to take advantage of the gentler grades they saw ahead of them, and wove from one side to the other rather than staying on a string-straight line.

Beneath the towering pines the ground was thick with saplings. Some were only shoots that fell short of being knee-high. Others had grown to be taller than the head of a man riding horseback. The tall saplings would survive and grow into loggable trees while the smaller shoots died for lack of the sunshine that the higher trees cut off from the ground.

Between the stands of pine, creeping blue-flowered vines grew in thick patches. These were columbines, which in the Shoshone language were called *i-de-heo,* and which had given the territory its name.

Here and there rock outcrops broke the surface. A few of these showed raw freshly exposed faces where the sampling picks of prospectors had chiped away at them in search of the dull grey veins of silver ore that they hoped would bring them riches. The broken rocks and the faintly marked trail were the only signs Jessie and Ki saw of man's intrusion into the wild land.

"Except for this old trail and those marks of prospector's picks, it looks like we could be the first people who ever saw this place, Ki," Jessie remarked as their horses plodded along the upslanting terrain. "I'm beginning to wonder if we might not be following the wrong trail."

"It was the only one we saw," Ki reminded her. "And the liveryman at Coeur d'Alene didn't mention another one."

"But if the story Congressman Dawson heard is true, and a bunch of outlaws are really building that town up on the Canadian border, they'd have to haul supplies in from Coeur d'Alene." Jessie frowned. "And this certainly isn't a wagon road that we're following now."

"That's true." Ki nodded. "But maybe they're getting their lumber and food from Canada."

"I suppose they could be." Jessie frowned. "But where in Canada? As far as I can remember, there's no large town along the border east of Vancouver except Calgary, and it's a hundred miles north of the Canadian line."

"We've certainly gone too far to turn back now," Ki said thoughtfully. "But we're not in any danger of getting lost. The liveryman seemed to know this country pretty well,

26

and I don't think we could possibly miss the landmarks he gave us."

"I'm sure you're right," Jessie agreed. "There's the big lake he told us to look for, Pend Oreille; and even if we managed to miss it somehow, he said we'd have a long day's ride along the lake shore until we reached the main river that feeds it. The Priest River, isn't it?"

Ki nodded. "We've got all the landmarks we need to get to the border, Jessie, and all of them are too big to miss. The best thing we can do is follow this trail—I suspect it's an old prospecting trail—until we hit one of them."

"Yes," Jessie agreed. "It's almost certain to be a prospecting trail, because once you get even a short distance off the trail, the ground's undisturbed. The only signs of prospecting are those broken rocks."

"If you're thinking that by now we might be on the land Alex bought, I'm inclined to agree with you," Ki nodded. "As far as I can remember, he never did look at it, just bought it to help one of his business associates who needed some ready money."

"I have been wondering about it," Jessie admitted.

"Somebody's been prospecting your land, though," Ki said. "If you noticed, all those pick marks we've seen are still fresh. The rocks that were broken haven't had time to weather yet."

"I don't like the idea of somebody prospecting on Starbuck land without me knowing about it, Ki, but I don't suppose whoever was looking for signs of silver ever bothered to find out who owned it."

"You needn't worry, Jessie," Ki told her. "Whoever did the prospecting went away disappointed. Those broken rocks we saw didn't have any silver veins in them, so we've probably passed the place where the ore deposits end."

"I'm just as glad, Ki," Jessie told him. "This country's too beautiful to be broken up by mining."

"We've still got a long way to go before we'll be off your land, though," Ki reminded her. "The land Alex bought runs from the southern end of Lake Pend Oreille all the way to the Canadian border."

"Yes, that is a long way," she agreed. "And this winding trail doesn't make it any shorter." After they'd ridden a few hundred yards further, she added, "You've led that packhorse since we stopped at noon, Ki. Do you want me to handle the lead rope for a while?"

"No. We agreed you'd lead it in the mornings and I'd take care of it the rest of the day," Ki told her. Then he suggested, "If you're getting tired, we can stop and camp for the night. Or we can stop at the first spring we come to, or even bear to the east and find Lake Pend Oreille."

"We've still got three more days of riding ahead of us, Ki," Jessie replied thoughtfully. "I'm not especially tired, but perhaps we had better ride in the direction of the lake and stop when we get to it."

Changing their course to angle away from the fast dropping sun, they rode another quarter of an hour before catching sight of the glint of blue water between the close-spaced trees.

"We've finally gotten to Lake Pend Oreille," Ki said as he pointed to the spot where the water showed.

"Are you sure, Ki?"

"Yes. It's been a long time since I came here with Alex, but Pend Oreille is the only large lake in this vicinity."

They angled toward the lake shore and turned to ride parallel to the water's edge. Now for the first time Jessie could get an idea of the full extent of the rippling expanse of blue water.

"Why—Lake Pend Oreille's huge!" Jessie exclaimed. "Why didn't you tell me how big it was, Ki?"

"I thought it'd be a nice surprise for you to find out for yourself," Ki replied. "I remember how I felt when Alex brought me here for the first time."

"It looks more like an ocean than a lake!"

Jessie was gazing across at the opposite shore as she spoke. The trees on the other side of the wide expanse of deep blue water seemed to be nothing more than tall bushes. She looked from one side to another, trying to see the ends of the lake, but the curving shoreline of the opposite bank hid the rest of it from sight.

"It's a big lake, all right," Ki agreed. "Alex guessed it to be about ten miles across and perhaps twenty miles from end to end. And it's all on your land, Jessie. I remember Alex making a remark to that effect after he'd inspected the property."

"It's too bad we don't have it on the Circle Star," Jessie said after a moment. "Compared to this, the waterholes there aren't any bigger than pinheads."

Ki smiled as he replied, "We'd never have to worry about having a dry year if we had the lake in Texas. But I'm afraid that if we did, we'd have a bunch of very jealous neighbors."

"And I couldn't find it in my heart to blame them," Jessie told him. "And that little cove we just passed looked so cool and inviting, I think I'm going to go back to it for a swim, as soon as we've found a place to camp."

"What's wrong with that spot just ahead of us?" Ki asked, pointing to an area where neither trees nor brush ran down to the water's edge.

"It looks good to me," Jessie agreed. "We'll unload the pack horse and set up camp, then I'll backtrack and have my swim."

"Why don't you just go back now, Jessie?" Ki suggested. "While you're in the water, I'll unload the pack horse and unsaddle the others. Then I'll dive in for a few minutes while you start supper."

"A good idea." She nodded. "All right, Ki. I'll ride back to that little bushy point and have my swim. Then I'll lead my horse back and save you the trouble of unsaddling him."

"You know I don't mind taking your saddle off, Jessie."

"Of course I do. But I'm going to change clothes when I get out of the water, and if I just ride on back I'll have my fresh outfit handy in my saddlebags. Besides, I'm impatient to get into that cool, clear water, now that I've seen it."

"Go ahead, then," Ki said. "And take your time. There's still almost an hour before sundown. While you're swimming I'll unpack the saddlebags and pick up some dry deadwood and start our supper fire."

"And you can swim while I cook supper," Jessie agreed.

She turned her horse, and when it neared the cove that had caught her eye, she reined the animal to angle toward the shoreline, fifty yards or so away. As she drew closer, she saw what had been invisible at a distance: a dense growth of pine saplings intertwined with vines that stretched back from the rippling surface.

Changing the angle of her approach to the shore, Jessie rode almost parallel to the water's edge, looking for a place where land and water met without a belt of tangled vegetation. After a few minutes she spotted the place she'd been seeking: a tiny indentation in the bank cove where a sandy edge of soil met the line at which the lake's clear water lapped with gentle persistence.

When she reached the spot she'd selected, Jessie reined in and dismounted. She tethered the horse and took fresh clothing from her saddlebags, hanging it across the branch of the small fir to which she'd tethered her horse. Hanging her gunbelt over her saddlehorn, she walked to the water's edge. The cool, glassy surface was rippling slightly in the late afternoon breeze, and she could see the sandy bottom that shelved out beneath the ripples. She undressed quickly, enjoying listening to the soft sussurrus of the glass-clear water as it washed against the small stretch of smooth beach sand.

When she walked out into the lake, the water was chilly at first, but the sensation of cold vanished when Jessie waded deeper. She swam away from shore a short distance, clumsy at first, since long months had passed since she'd been in the water. Then the knack of timing her movements returned to her, and she swam easily, moving now as though the water were her natural habitat.

Enjoying thoroughly her first swim in many long months, Jessie swam back and forth for a while, then fishtailed in the water, her muscular arms pulling her below the surface. She opened her eyes and found that she could see almost as well as she could when looking through the air.

Suddenly she saw the silvery flash of a trout turning, and started to swim after it. Then she thought better of it as she realized how deep the water was, only a few dozen yards from the shore. She swam for a little while longer, her muscles attuned to the new element now, and suddenly realized that she'd been in the water for a long while and that Ki had been waiting to have his own swim.

Regretfully, she returned to shore. By now the sun was touching the tops of the tall pines that rose on the lake's opposite shore. The cooling breezes that in the mountains of the Western high country always warned of the beginning dusk were riffling the waters of the lake. Jessie was shivering in the breeze by the time she reached the fresh clothing she'd laid over the top of a small pine near the water's edge, and she dressed hurriedly.

Feeling thoroughly refreshed now as well as warmed, she swung into the saddle of the livery horse and started back to where she'd left Ki. The air was fast getting cooler, and the first hint of twilight was showing in the deep blue sky above the thick growth of trees that lined the shore.

Riding in a shallow arc to avoid the tangled brush that began at the water's edge and extended back along the bank for several dozen yards, Jessie rode back to the point where she'd turned to the cove, and then reined her horse back toward the shoreline. She saw no sign either of Ki or the horses between her and the clear area that stretched to the water's edge. A puzzled frown grew on her face. The frown grew deeper as she reined the horse to move parallel

31

to the shoreline and after several minutes of forward progress still saw no sign of Ki.

Reining in, Jessie scanned the terrain. Slowly, signs that she noticed only subconsciously when she and Ki had chosen the spot for their overnight camp registered on her mind.

There was a broken branch dangling from one of the tall pines that she now recalled having noticed. An oddly shaped clump of brush at one end of the clear shoreline had also registered in her memory. Touching her horse's flank with the toe of her boot, Jessie reined the animal down to the water's edge. Now she was surer than before that she hadn't been mistaken, for the prints of Ki's sandals were clear in the soft ground where the water lapped the earth.

Very concerned now, Jessie dismounted and dropped the reins of the livery horse to the ground so the animal would stand still. Her eyes fixed on the ground, she walked back and forth along the lake shore, examining the ground. It was scuffed by hoofprints at the spot where Ki had been tethering the horses when she'd left for her swim. A pile of dark, fresh dung showed that the animals had been tied there for a little while, at least.

Then Jessie saw the boot print. Her puzzlement turned to worry. She moved to the print and examined it closely. There was nothing to note, other than that the man who'd left the print in the spot of soft soil had moved around a bit, but the scuffed earth bore too many half oblitered prints of horses' hooves and Ki's sandals to allow Jessie to form a clear picture of the man's movements.

Jessie had been in too many crisis situations to let panic grow and obscure her judgment. Methodically, she began ranging a bit more widely over the area she and Ki had chosen for their overnight camp.

Away from the water's edge, the ground was too hard or was covered too thickly with short, curled grasses to take and hold either footprints or hoofprints. The occasional prints that Jessie found gave her no clues as to the identity of the man whose bootprint she'd found where the horses were tethered, or to his movements. Ki's soft sandals with their foot-fitting soles seemed to have left no prints other than those she'd seen in the moist earth near the water's edge.

Both baffled and angry, Jessie stopped beside her horse and looked at the sky. During the time she'd spent trying to find footprints in the little clearing, twilight had advanced. The sky that was visible overhead above the clearing was already taking on the deep blue hue of night. Shadows were forming under the thick-growing pines along the shoreline, and the water of the lake was taking on the black sheen it wore during the hours of darkness.

Jessie had realized some minutes earlier that someone, a man, had managed to surprise Ki and take him captive. How this had been done was still a mystery; so was the reason why. Now, she reached a quick conclusion. To try to track Ki and his captor would be impossible, a sheer waste of time in the fast-settling darkness. She had no idea who might have managed the deed, for with his mastery of Oriental hand combat, Ki was not one who could be subdued easily.

There was only one way to resolve Jessie's dilemma, and she took it at once. Tethering the horse, she unsaddled it and spread her bedroll a short distance away from it. With her Colt within quick grasping distance and her rifle along the side of her bedroll, Jessie lay down without undressing. Her stomach was protesting, but all the food she and Ki had brought was in the load carried by their packhorse.

Looking up at the sky, dark now above the tips of the tall pines, Jessie studied the stars and cudgeled her brain for an answer to the mystery of Ki's capture, until at last she went to sleep.

Chapter 4

Jessie's sleep that night was light and restless. She was awakened several times by the rustling of the trees and bushes when the wind gusted briefly, and each time a night noise aroused her, she sat up in her blankets, her hand reaching for her Colt in a reflex that was by now almost instinctive. All the night's disturbances had proved to be false alarms. After she'd been roused from a fitful slumber a half-dozen times by the same kinds of sounds, Jessie became able to identify them for what they were, and ignore them.

During the brief moments when she was trying to summon sleep to return, she tried to free her mind of worry by identifying the night noises as they recurred. One was the thudding, raspy sound mady by two tree limbs coming together when stirred by a breeze coming from a certain direction. Another she identified as the whispery rasp of some close-rooted saplings rubbing when the wind veered to a different angle. The *hush-hush* of tall weeds swaying was harder to identify, but she readily recognized the splash of a night-feeding trout falling back into the water after it had jumped to engulf an insect floating on the lake's surface.

Daybreak finally began to lighten the eastern horizon-line, and when habit and hunger combined to awaken her fully, Jessie slipped out of the coccoon of her blankets and began searching the ground around the shore.

This time, with the sky brightening instead of fading, she discovered what she'd been unable to see the evening before. Near the extreme edge of the little clearing she and Ki had chosen for their campsite she discovered three sets of footprints along the shoreline, some of them even beyond the shore, covered by inch-deep water.

As Jessie studied the footprints she could see that two sets of the prints had been made by the unknown intruder. One set marked his approach, the other his departure after he'd made Ki his prisoner. The man had worn boots with caulk-studded soles, a sign that he was or had been a lumberjack.

Superimposed on the first set of footprints was a second set made by the caulk-booted stranger; these marked his departure. His departing prints were paralleled by a line of prints made by Ki's flat-soled sandals. Both trails were at the water's edge, and sometimes under the inches-deep water. As the sky brightened with the swift approach of sunlight Jessie could see still more when she stared through the shallows beyond the shoreline. There, she could make out the deep, round impressions left by the hooves of Ki's horse and the pack horse.

Given the footprints and hoofprints, Jessie could re-create immediately what must have happened while she was swimming the evening before. At some time shortly after she got beyond earshot of the spot she and Ki had chosen for their overnight camp, the intruder had sneaked up to the spot along the shoreline. Shielded by the growth of saplings and water-weeds that came down to the water's edge, he'd reached the little clearing without Ki having heard or seen him.

That the man who wore hobnail boots had taken Ki by surprise was equally obvious. Since the ground at the water's edge was undisturbed, Jessie was sure that the unknown intruder had been able to approach in silence and hold Ki at gunpoint before Ki could move with his customary lightning speed.

Although Jessie admitted to herself that her deductions were largely guesswork, she surmised that a much trodden spot at the shoreline where the unknown's footprints and Ki's overlapped and created a confusion of intermingled depressions had been the place where Ki had been forced to stand while his captor tied his hands.

Holding Ki at gunpoint then, the stranger had forced Ki, leading the horses, to walk ahead of him in the shallows off the shoreline. Ki's surprise must have been complete, for no signs in the three sets of footprints showed that Ki had at any time been able to launch a counterattack.

Jessie read an invisible message from Ki carried by the visible evidence. Understanding her companion as well as she did, she was sure that at some point during his encounter with the intruding stranger Ki had seen an opportunity to launch a *seiken* attack against the mysterious man who had taken him prisoner. Following this line of thought, Jessie became convinced that Ki had had very good reasons for failing to do so, and that he had equally good reasons for failing to use his *shuriken* blades against the threat of his captor's gun.

There was only one reason that Jessie could see for Ki's restraint: He'd grasped the opportunity to uncover an outlaw hideout by allowing himself to be captured, positive that Jessie would follow him. Without wasting time by examining the footprints further, Jessie swung into the saddle of the livery horse and reined it to the shallows at the water's edge.

By this time the sky had brightened to full daybreak and

the sun was sending its shining rays slanting through the tops of the tall pines across the lake. The lake's bottom was now clearly visible through the crystalline shallows along the bank, where the water was only a few inches deep. Jessie had no trouble following the hoofprints and footprints that pocked the lake bottom.

For a half-mile or more, the round depressions in the soft ocher earth led her along the bank. Then they slanted toward the shore. On the firmer grass-coated soil that began a short distance from the water's edge, the prints of Ki's sandals and the hobnail-studded boots of his captor both disappeared. The hoofprints of the horses were still plain, however. Jessie realized that they'd now mounted the horses instead of leading them. She set out to follow them.

After she'd covered almost two miles, she had to cross a stretch of earth covered heavily with shore-weeds and pine needles where the prints vanished almost completely. Jessie persevered, holding her mount to a slow walk, but there came a time when she realized that she'd seen no hoofprints for some time. Knowing that she must have overrun the point where they turned away from the lake, Jessie turned back.

Several minutes of scouting around put her back on the trail once more, but now Ki and his captor had headed away from the soft, slanting ground that led down to the lake shore. They were riding across firmer soil where the horses' hooves made little imprint, and from that time on Jessie's progress became much slower. There were spots where she lost the trail completely, and had to scout in a series of zigzags while riding slowly ahead until she crossed the tracks again.

As the morning wore on, Jessie's empty stomach began to protest. All the food that she and Ki had brought for their trip was in the panniers carried by the pack horse. Jessie had not eaten since noon of the day before, when she and Ki had halted for a noontime snack, and by now the

38

sun was climbing high toward its zenith. Ignoring the silent nagging of her hunger, Jessie kept moving ahead. The knowledge that she was ten to twelve hours behind Ki and the man who was holding him prisoner gave her an urgency that could not be ignored.

When Jessie saw the faint traces of a beaten pathway ahead, her spirits soared briefly and then sank. Until now, she'd managed with very little trouble to make out the hoofprints of the three horses that she'd set out to follow. The presence of even a seldom travelled road tipped the scales against her, though. She had no assurance that on a path used by others she could distinguish the three sets of hoofprints that Ki, his captor, and the pack horse had left.

Reaching the faintly marked pathway, Jessie reined in while she looked along it in both directions. Just as she'd thought might be the case, the almost invisible trace was pocked by a half-dozen sets of hoofprints as well as rutted by the wheels of wagons. On the surface of the beaten pathway one set of hoofprints looked no different than another.

Dropping her horse's reins over its neck, Jessie dismounted to examine the road's surface more closely. When seen from her saddle, the narrow, beaten path had shown the marks of a half-dozen sets of hoofprints, but at closer range it showed still more. Even a few yards from where Ki and his captor had taken to the road she could not distinguish the hoofmarks of Ki's horse or the stranger's horse or the pack-horse.

Holding her feeling of angry frustration in check, Jessie looked along the road in both directions. She saw nothing but the landscape when she gazed down the deserted trace in the direction from which she and Ki had travelled to the lake, but when she looked north the glint of bright metal caught her eyes at once.

For a moment Jessie stared at the gleam, unable to make out what it was. Then she slitted her eyes to reduce the amount of light entering them from the bright sun. This increased her ability to see, for the sun was almost directly overhead by this time, and partly closing her eyes caused her pupils to dilate slightly. Now, Jessie was almost positive that she could identify the gleaming object that was catching the rays of the sun, for she could see that it had a man-made shape. Its circular formation was not one usually found in objects created by nature.

Mounting her horse again, Jessie rode slowly toward the shining dot. It grew more plainly visible as she drew closer to it, and even before she reined in beside it Jessie had confirmed her first tentative identification. The shining piece of metal that had caught her glance was one of the brightly polished steel *shuriken* blades that Ki always carried in a leather case strapped to his wrist.

As Jessie drew closer, she could see that the *shuriken* was sticking upright, partly embedded in the earth beside the road. She realized instantly that its position could not possibly be an accident, for if the thin metal throwing-blade had simply fallen from the leather case in which Ki carried the weapons it would be lying flat and almost invisible on the ground.

There was only one reason she could think of to explain its presence. Ki must have found an opportunity to launch the weapon in a throw that would cause it to lodge it upright in the firm soil bordering the road. Suddenly the embedded *shuriken* became a crystal clear message that Ki had managed to leave for her; one that was as clear to Jessie as it would have been if Ki had been there to give it to her in his own words. Somehow, he'd managed to slip the *shuriken* out of the leather case strapped to his left forearm and toss it there to mark the direction in which his captor was taking him.

Jessie dismounted long enough to pull the *shuriken* from the soil and put it in one of her saddle bags. Then she remounted quickly and continued following the trail, keeping her eyes on the roadside for another of Ki's silent but eloquent messages.

Although Jessie watched carefully as she rode, she did not find another *shuriken* until the day was almost over. The sun was dipping low in the western sky and she'd almost given up hope of seeing another of the metal blades when she spotted the weapon's bright gleam. This *shuriken* was on the left hand side of the road, where she could not see it until she was almost directly in line with it.

Like the first blade had been, the sharp cutting edge of this one was deeply embedded in the hard, sunbaked dirt beside the road. Jessie was quick to note that not only was it on the side of the road opposite that on which she'd found the first one, but that it was a long three paces from the road itself.

As she gazed at it, a frown grew on Jessie's face. She knew how accurately Ki could hit a target with a *shuriken*, and told herself at once that Ki must have had a reason for embedding the blade in the soil where it now rested.

Dismounting again, Jessie walked across the road and stood beside the newly discovered *shuriken* for a moment. As she raised her head, puzzling over the reason for the blade's position, she caught sight of the bright glint of a second blade even further from the road. She started toward it, and as she walked slowly up the slope from the road she saw for the first time the freshly scuffed soil ahead.

When she reached the *shuriken* she could also see the hoofprints of the three horses on an almost invisible trail a few feet away from the embedded blade. Ki's reason for placing the second *shuriken* where she'd found it was clear to Jessie now. His captor had turned off the main road, and was taking Ki on the almost obliterated trace that led up the sloping side of the range of low hills rising west of Lake Pend Oreille.

Stopping only long enough to pull the *shuriken* from the

41

hard soil, Jessie retraced her footsteps. She stopped on the down-slope long enough to retrieve the *shuriken* that had caught her attention first, and continued down the slope to her horse. She put the two blades in her saddlebag with the first one, then mounted and reined her horse up the slope, following the faintly marked branch trail in the gathering dusk.

Jessie's empty stomach kept reminding her how hungry she was as she peered through the increasingly dim light at the faint trail she was following up the steeply slanting flanks of the Selkirk Mountains.

Here the forest had not been reached by the lumbermen of an advancing civilization, and the towering white pines grew close together. The big trees, untouched by axe or saw, forced travellers to follow a sinuous path that wound in and out between their boles. It was a trail that would have been hard enough to follow in daylight, and by now the spreading branches overlapped and often intertwined to keep the ground in deep shadow.

Ignoring the urgings of her empty stomach, Jessie pressed on as best she could. Her livery horse was tiring now, and its progress was too slow to suit her, but she was wise enough about the habits of horses to let the animal set its own slow pace as it carried her up the almost invisible trail that wove in and out between the pines.

Only the slightest tinge of daylight remained in the sky that was intermittently visible through the interwoven branches when Jessie saw the faint flicker of firelight ahead. In that moment she was glad for the dusk, and for the closely spaced treetrunks. In cleared land she could not possibly have reached her goal without her approach having been detected long ago.

At her sight of the first gleam of firelight, Jessie reined in the livery horse. She sat quietly in the saddle, straining her ears, but she was still too far away to hear anything that was being said by whoever had kindled the fire. She slipped out of her saddle and knotted the horse's reins around the nearest sapling. Pulling her rifle from its saddle scabbard, she moved with silent caution toward the red gleam of firelight.

"What the hell are we gonna have to do to make this Chinee son of a bitch talk?" a rough voice grated into the forest's silence. "He ain't said a word or answered any question I ast him since I taken his gag off. Come down to it, he didn't even say nothing when I snagged him down there by the big lake."

Jessie stopped at once behind the first tree big enough to shield her. She could not see Ki or his captors, but she was close enough to the fire to hear the men around it clearly.

"Maybe we better slap him around a little bit, Frisco," a second voice replied. It was as gratingly harsh and unfeeling as the first man's had been. The speaker went on. "I'll bet he'll talk fast enough if you do that."

"I got a better idea, Moose," the man addressed as Frisco replied. "I didn't have time to waste and get here before dark, so I ain't tried it yet, but I say we take them sandals off of him and toast his feet. I ain't run into nobody that'd stay clammed up when their feet begun to get blistered."

"Now, that's the idee, Frisco!" Moose agreed. "He damn sure ain't just no Chinee laundryman, not with all the grub and the other truck he's got stuffed into them panniers on that pack horse."

"That's sorta how I figgered," Frisco went on. "But he sure as hell don't run with our bunch, because he ain't packing iron, even if there was a coupla boxes of rifle and pistol shells in the pack horse's load."

"Well, he can't be such a much," a third voice chimed in. "I say we give him another chance to talk; and if he don't, the best thing to do is get rid of him right here and now."

"How about it, you Chink bastard?" Moose asked. "You gonna tell us who you are and where you're heading, or do we have to get it outta you the hard way?"

43

"Now, wait a minute!" Frisco broke in. "I just thought about something. Didn't Clutch say he'd put out the word that he was looking for girls up at the new town? That's the only place this fellow could be heading for, and if we toast his feet or anything like that, it'll be our butts when Clutch hears about what we done."

"Who says Clutch has to find out?" the third voice asked, his voice challenging. "He might be the boss in town, but that don't give him nothing here. I'll say it again. Give the Chink one more chance to talk, and get rid of him if he don't."

"Platz here has got the idee," Moose agreed. "Then we'll cut cards for his horses and gear and whatever's in them saddlebags."

Jessie had been cudgelling her brain, trying to think of a way to free Ki without risking his death before she succeeded in getting him out of his captors' reach. Certain that the men would have their attention riveted on Ki, she stepped from her cover and moved closer to them. As she moved she looked for another tree that she could use as a shield. Before she could select one, Platz spoke again.

"All right, Chink," he said.

Jessie glanced at the fire again and saw that Platz had moved to stand directly in front of Ki.

"You got one last chance," Platz went on. "But I guess if you understand English, you already heard what we was saying. We're smart enough to know that nobody comes this way without a reason. Now, who in hell sent you kiting up this way? Where're you heading and why?"

"My reason for being here is as good as yours," Ki replied. "And I would advise you to release me before Clutch gets angry with you for stopping me."

"You know Clutch?" Platz challenged.

"Would I be going to see him if I didn't?" Ki retorted.

"Then tell me what he looks like," Platz went on. "Because I think you're lying. You just picked up what we was saying and you're trying to pull a bluff to save your skin."

"By God, Platz is right!" Frisco said loudly. "If that son-of-a-bitching yellowbelly had been looking for the town, he'd've asked me how to find it!"

"Let's get rid of him right now, then!" Moose said, his voice rising to a half shout.

Jessie saw Moose's hand drop to the butt of his holstered pistol. Frisco was also moving now, stepping up to Ki as his hand moved toward his holstered weapon.

Jessie saw at once that she had no choice. Moose was already drawing, and she chose him for her first target. Her rifle cracked and its slug went home. Sure of her aim, Jessie did not wait to see if Moose went down, but swung the Winchester's muzzle toward Frisco, who'd switched his attention away from Ki when Jessie's shot rang out.

Jessie pumped a fresh shell into her Winchester. As she moved and fired, Frisco swung his pistol toward her. He swayed, held himself on his feet for a split second, then lurched and fell lifeless across Moose's body.

Platz was just turning away from Ki when Jessie's first shot broke up the outlaws' plans. Jessie fired as Platz raised his revolver. The outlaw's finger tightened on the trigger in his dying reflex, but the weapon was already sagging in his hand and its slug did nothing but kick up a puff of forest duff as it sped into the ground.

Then the echoes of the gunfire faded and the little grove was silent.

Chapter 5

"I'd say you got here just in time, Jessie," Ki commented calmly as the last echo of the gunfire faded into silence.

Without taking her eyes off the three figures that sprawled motionless around the fire, Jessie replied, "I'm afraid it took me a long time, Ki. And I didn't really want to shoot those men. I was hoping I'd be able to hold them at gunpoint while I got you free."

"There'd have been shooting sooner or later," Ki told her. "They were real hard-case killers. I overheard enough of their talk to find that out."

"But I'd really planned to take them alive. I'm sure they could've answered a lot of questions that I wanted to ask."

"You must've been close enough to hear them talking about what to do with me," Ki said. When Jessie nodded, he added, "Then we both know now that the rumor we came to investigate seems to be true."

"It convinced me, Ki."

"Yes. And I was already half-convinced. After hearing

47

what they said, I'm sure that there really is an outlaw town being started up on the Canadian border. And I'm ready to go looking for it, but there's not much I can do until you relieve me of these handcuffs."

"I'm sorry, Ki!" Jessie exclaimed. "I should've done that the first thing! Which one of them had the key?"

With a gesture of his head, Ki indicated Frisco's body. "He's the one who brought me here." As Jessie began searching the dead outlaw's pockets, Ki went on, "I hope my little guideposts helped you find me."

"They certainly did!" Jessie assured him as she stood up, the handcuff key in her hand. "I almost missed seeing the first one, because a *shuriken* was the last thing I'd expected to see up here in Idaho. After I saw it, I watched for more. And by the way, I picked up those you threw and saved them for you."

"I was pretty sure you would," Ki nodded as Jessie unlocked the handcuffs. "I'll get them from you later."

"How on earth did you manage to throw those *shuriken* while you were handcuffed, and with that outlaw watching you?" Jessie asked.

"He wasn't watching me every minute of the time," Ki said as he rubbed his wrists. "And you've had handcuffs on, Jessie. You know they leave your hands reasonably free. But I couldn't move fast enough or throw hard enough to be sure I'd put him out of commission with my first blade."

"You knew I'd be following you as soon as I got back to camp and found you missing, I suppose?"

Ki nodded. "Of course. And I feel like a careless fool for letting that fellow Frisco take me prisoner."

"How did he manage to bring it off?"

"He moved more silently than any man I've ever encountered, Jessie. I was hunkered down at the edge of the lake, washing, and he sneaked up behind me and shoved me into the lake. I just couldn't get any footing on that slippery mud bottom. He was holding his gun on me when

48

I got on my feet, and made me stay in the water until he'd handcuffed me."

"Then you were handcuffed all the time?"

Ki nodded. "But after we'd started I managed to mark our trail by spinning them blades into the ground when he wasn't looking."

After a moment's pause, Jessie asked, "Well, now that we're together again, I'm only worried about one thing, Ki."

"What's that?"

"Even if we're sure this new hideout's getting started, we still don't know where it is."

"There can't be too many towns this far north in Idaho," Ki told her. "We shouldn't have much trouble finding it."

"I hope you're right," Jessie said. "But we'll worry about that in the morning. Right now, I've suddenly remembered how hungry I am. All I can think of is eating."

"Of course!" Ki said. "All our food's on the pack horse. It's tethered with the outlaws' animals, right behind that stand of trees."

"I know we've got some cheese," Jessie went on. "And I'll settle for a bite of that while we're deciding what we want to do. Later we can have a real meal."

While Ki was getting the cheese for her, Jessie looked around the little clearing. Except for the three corpses, it seemed as suitable a spot as any to spend the night, and when Ki returned she suggested that they stay there.

"I don't see any real reason to move," he agreed. "I'll drag those bodies into the brush, and then build up the fire. We'll want to cook something for supper too, but the cheese will keep you from starving while we're busy."

Jessie was chewing, so she nodded in reply. When she'd swallowed the big bite of cheese, she said, "One of the first things we need to do is go through the saddlebags that belonged to those outlaws. If we're lucky, we'll find letters or papers of some kind that might give us a hint of what to look for and what to expect when and if we find that out-

49

law town that Congressman Dawson was so concerned about."

Ki nodded. "Yes. But supper comes first, Jessie. I'm hungry as a wolf myself. I'll clear up around the fire, and then we can take our time doing the rest of it."

"It can't be very much farther," Ki told Jessie. "Unless we've misread that map we found in Platz's saddlebags."

Four days had passed since their encounter with the outlaws. Half of the first day had been lost while Ki buried the dead men and Jessie went through the outlaws' saddlebags. Her search had produced only one useful item, a rough sketch map that they'd decided must have some special significance, for it was the only document among the scanty personal possessions of any of the trio.

When they'd finally set out late in the morning they'd followed the hit-and-miss trail that wound along the western bank of Lake Pend Oreille, and forded the Priest River at the head of the lake. Then, guided by the dead outlaw's map they'd reached the Kootenai River after another day and a half of easy riding.

To their surprise, a cable ferryboat was operating, and it took them across the wide rough stream. The ferryman, a grizzled man who could have been any age above sixty, had been singularly uncommunicative. He'd kept busy hauling the narrow, scowlike boat across the river, and had answered most of their questions with either a headshake or a nod, or with a question of his own.

"Where you people heading for?" he'd asked when Jessie tried to get the locations of the towns north of the Kootenai River.

"We're looking for a new town to the east," Jessie had replied. "I don't even know whether it has a name yet."

"New town?" the ferryman had responded, shooting a stream of tobacco juice into the river without missing a single hand-over-hand tug at the cable. "Ain't no sich animule. Not this side of Medicine Hat, anyways."

"How far is that?" Jessie had asked.

"Nigh on to a week's steady riding."

"And there's no town between?" Ki put in.

"None I ever heerd of," the grizzled oldster had replied. "Now, if you was looking to go to Calgary, you'd just keep on heading north. Was you going to Vancouver, I'd say to take the first left hand fork in the road up ahead. But whichever way you're heading, there ain't no towns to speak of."

"What is there to the east?" Jessie asked.

"Mountains and plenty of 'em. Turn right at the second fork if it's Medicine Hat you're aiming for. There ain't but the one way to git there."

After they'd left the ferry, Jessie said to Ki, "You know, I don't believe that man was telling us the truth about there not being any towns except Medicine Hat east of here."

"He did seem a bit uncomfortable when we asked about towns to the east," Ki nodded. "He certainly changed the subject awfully fast."

"Let's push ahead, then," Jessie said decisively. "It wouldn't surprise me if Platz or somebody in cahoots with him had paid that old ferryman to keep quiet."

Ki nodded. "Stranger things have happened. We can cover a lot of ground in a day or two, and if we don't find the town we're looking for, all we can do is turn back."

Though they did not push their horses, they covered a good many miles over the gently rolling forest land during the afternoon and morning they travelled after leaving the ferry. As they rode eastward, the trees began to thin and the land changed almost mile by mile from forest to semi-arid desert.

"Suppose we give ourselves today and half of tomorrow," Jessie suggested as she and Ki left their overnight camp. "I still think that map we found is right."

"It isn't much of a map," Ki reminded her. "Just a few pretty badly scrawled lines."

"I'm surprised we found one," Jessie replied. "You

51

know how most lawbreakers are; they hate to put anything in writing because they're always afraid it might be brought up in court as evidence."

"We'd probably feel the same way if we were outlaws."

"I suppose we would. But if I were an outlaw and wanted to build a hideout where men dodging the law felt safe, this is just the kind of place I'd look for," Jessie went on. "We haven't seen a farm or a ranch or even a building of any kind or any other people on this trail since yesterday, when we left the ferry crossing."

Ki nodded and answered, "Yes. The farther we travel, the less anybody seems to know about this place we're looking for."

"That's one reason I'm inclined to think the map's right, though, Ki," Jessie went on. "People who'd be interested in the kind of place this mysterious town's supposed to be wouldn't do a lot of talking about it."

"True enough," Ki agreed. "And it wouldn't be the first secret hideout outlaws have built. The Hole in the Wall over in Wyoming Territory, Robber's Roost down in Montana, and that outlaw hideout we found in the canyon in Arizona—"

"I know," Jessie broke in, nodding. "And I'm sure there are a lot more we've never even heard about."

"About all we can do is keep looking, I suppose," Ki said. "If we don't find it over the top of this rise—" He stopped as they reached the crest of a long slope and looked down into the little semicircular valley that opened below them. "But it looks to me like we have."

He and Jessie reined in on the edge of the valley and sat silently, gazing down into it.

Below them the trail zigzagged down the slope that led to a shallow, curving valley. In the bottom of the hollow formed by the slopes of the surrounding hills, eight or ten large, unpainted wooden buildings formed a double row, facing each other across a slightly crooked, unpaved street. Only one of them looked anything but makeshift. This was a large two-story farmhouse, set apart from the others on the far side of the valley. The house stood out from the rest because of its shining white paint and green-shuttered windows. Alone among the others, it looked as though it had been built to endure.

Between the large, white house and the spot where Jessie and Ki were sitting on their horses, the buildings that lined the straggling main street of the settlement were spaced far apart, and in the spaces between many of them tents had been set up. Hitchrails stood in front of most of these, but only a few horses were tied to them.

On each side of the double row of permanent looking structures that formed the town's core, there were houses, perhaps fifteen or twenty on each side. They were all small and of uniform construction, spaced at random and set apart from one another. Mixed in with the houses were still more tents. These were smaller than the tents along the town's single street.

Many of the houses and tents that stood off the street faced in different directions, or stood at odd angles to one another. Aside from the street formed by the two rows of larger and more imposing structures, the settlement had no apparent pattern.

Four or five men were visible, walking along the street or roaming around in the open areas where houses and tents stood. Most of them seemed to be heading toward the settlement's one street, but none of them appeared to be in a hurry to complete whatever errand had brought them out.

Jessie finally broke the silence. "I was sure that old ferryman was lying to us, Ki," she said quietly. "This has to be the place we've been looking for. It's obviously a new town."

"It's a lot more of a town than I expected," Ki said, his eyes still fixed on the gaggle of buildings.

"I didn't really know what to expect," Jessie told him. "But I certainly didn't think it would be anything like this."

"Neither did I," Ki agreed. "Apparently Dawson didn't

53

know how busy the outlaws have been or how long they must have been working."

"They've been busy, all right," Jessie agreed. "And they must have been at it for quite a while. Think of all the trouble we've had getting here, and imagine how much longer we'd have taken if we'd been hauling a wagon loaded with lumber."

"Yes," Ki nodded, looking over the crescent-shaped valley. "It's really isolated. Things can happen here that nobody would ever know about. Whoever had the idea of building a town for outlaws here certainly picked a good location."

"But Congressman Dawson was right about it being a town, and that gives me the idea that he was probably right about it being an outlaw hideout."

"We'll find out soon enough," Ki said. "Now that we've found the place, I suppose we'd better ride on in and take a closer look at it."

Jessie nodded and touched the flank of her horse with the toe of her boot. The animal moved ahead. Ki followed. The horses carried them stiff-legged down the steep slope to the floor of the valley, and on into the town.

Seen at close range, the little settlement looked even more ramshackle than it had from the valley's rim. Only a few of the wooden buildings had been built with new lumber, and they were the shacks that stretched away from both sides of the town's only real street. The larger structures on the street itself showed signs that they'd been torn down at some previous location and the boards reassembled in the valley.

Only three or four of the larger buildings bore signs and these were surprisingly uniform. All but two of them had signs reading SALOON across their facades. The exceptions were one which identified itself as STULDEY'S TAVERN and another at the far end of the jagged street which bore a sign, GENERAL STORE, over an abbreviated roof extension that sheltered the doorway. Tacked to one of the posts supporting the overhang was another, smaller sign, hand-lettered in pencil on a square of cardboard. It read FRESH MEAT EVERY OTHER TUESDAY.

"It looks like this is the best place for us to ask a few questions," Jessie told Ki as they passed it. "Even in a town like this one, I don't think I'd be exactly welcome in one of those saloons."

"You're probably right," Ki nodded. "And since we've got to start somewhere, we might as well go in."

There was the usual hitchrail in front of the store. Jessie and Ki looped the reins of their horses over it and went inside. A bell tied by a thong to the entrance door jingled as they entered and stood blinking their eyes to adjust them to the dim interior light.

Two long wooden counters formed an aisle down the center of the building. A few bolts of cloth, a box containing spools of thread, and small stand displaying carded buttons stood on one of the counters. The other was bare, but behind it, floor-to-ceiling shelves held a scanty array of airtights with gaudy red and green labels identifying their contents. A battered chopping block was at the far end behind the counter. There were no clerks in sight, but a curtained doorway at the end of the aisle hinted that the store's attendants might be in a back room.

As Jessie and Ki started down the aisle, the curtains parted and woman appeared. After a second glance at her, Jessie decided she was in early middle age, judging by her hair, which bore no trace of grey. Her face was a bit drawn. Her eyes blinked as though the bell had disturbed a nap.

"Do something for you folks?" she asked.

"We'll need some groceries," Jessie told her. "But before we start looking around, perhaps you could tell us exactly where we are."

"You mean you don't know?" the woman asked.

"How could we?" Ki countered. "There wasn't a sign at the edge of town giving its name, and our map doesn't show a town anywhere near here."

"I guess that's on account of nobody's figured out what to call the place yet," the woman said. "We keep asking Dutch when he's going to name it, but he don't seem to be in no hurry."

"Dutch?" Jessie frowned.

"Dutch Ventner," the woman replied. "It was Dutch that built this place, and he claims he's got the right to name it, so I guess it's going to be him that'll have the say."

"This Dutch Ventner lives here, then?" Ki asked.

"Oh, sure. He makes a lot of trips, though," the woman said. "If you're looking for him, I can't say whether he's around right now or not."

"We're not looking for him or anybody else," Jessie said quickly. "We're just passing through, and this seemed to be a good place to stop for supplies and perhaps to rest a day or two before we go on."

"Well, you go ahead and tell me what you need," the woman told Jessie. "I'll be glad to—"

She stopped short as a man pushed through the curtained doorway at the end of the aisle. He moved slowly and with great difficulty, supporting himself with a cane in each hand. He could have been any age from forty to sixty. His hair was gray, and there was a gray, grizzled two-day stubble on his creased cheeks and jutting chin. He was a broad shouldered man who'd once stood straight and tall, but whose shoulders now sagged, as did his belly. He looked at Jessie and blinked, his blue eyes narrowing, then opening wide.

"I was sure I hadn't forgot them voices I kept hearing!" he exclaimed. "Jessie! Jessie Starbuck! And Ki! Of all the people I never looked to see in this place!"

"Sid?" Jessie frowned as she studied the man's face. "Sid Bennet?"

"I see you ain't forgot," Bennett said, limping down the center aisle toward Jessie and Ki. "Even if it's been a while since I foremanned for your daddy on the Circle Star."

"It's been a good spell of years," Ki put in as he stepped

down the aisle to meet Bennet. The two men shook hands. "A lot's happened since you left the ranch."

"I reckon," Bennet agreed. He turned to Jessie and went on soberly, "I heard about your daddy being killed, but I was up in Montana Territory by then, and it'd been a good spell before the news got up there. Wasn't any way for me to tell you how sorry I was, Jessie. Then I moved on, over to the Black Hills and then to Bozeman and a lot of other places."

Jessie nodded. "I understand. But it's good to see you again, Sid."

"And the same goes double for me, Jessie!" Bennet told her. "And then me and Annie here met up and got hitched, and my legs kept getting tremblier, so I quit ranch-handing and taken to storekeeping, and now me and Annie's wound up here."

"In a new town that doesn't even have a name yet," Jessie smiled.

Bennet's smile faded and his face grew sober. "It's that, all right. And a lot more besides. And I don't know what you and Ki are doing here, but take an old man's advice and move on as fast as you can!"

"What're you telling me, Sid!" she asked.

"This town ain't no place for a proper lady like you to be, Jessie!" he said soberly. "I oughta keep my mouth shut if I know what's good for me, but you two buy what you need and get out just as quick as you can, before you get into the kind of trouble that ain't easy to fix."

Chapter 6

For a moment Jessie stared at Bennet, her eyes widening and a frown growing on her face. Then she said, "Maybe you'd better explain what you mean, Sid. You see, this is the place Ki and I started out to find."

"Are you telling me you heard about it all the way back in Texas?" Bennet asked.

"Not quite in Texas," Ki said quickly. "Jessie and I started here from San Francisco."

"San Francisco or Texas, it don't much matter, Ki," the old man told him. "Both of 'em's a long ways off. Why, there's folks living a heap closer to here that don't know about this town yet."

"Perhaps I'd better explain," Jessie said. "Ki and I came here to find out whether this town was real or just a lot of rumor and idle talk."

"Oh, it's real, all right," Annie broke in. "If you don't believe what you're looking at with your own two eyes, me and Sid can tell you."

59

"Sure we can, Annie," Sid said. "But if you remember, we didn't think it was ever going to be real when Dutch first begun talking to us about how he had in mind to set up a place like this."

"What do you mean 'a place like this'?" Jessie frowned.

"Never mind about the kind of place it is right now," Bennet told her. "What I'm aiming at is to find out how you and Ki got onto the town being here, wherever you was."

"You must've heard of Congressman Dawson," Jessie said, and when Bennet nodded she went on. "He's the one who asked Ki and me to come up here and take a look. He'd heard about a new town being started up and was ... well, he was curious about it, since it was supposed to be in Idaho Territory."

"And that's the size of it?" Bennet asked.

Before she answered, Jessie glanced at Ki. When he shrugged, she turned back to the old storekeeper and said, "No. It's not quite everything, Sid. The congressman had heard some gossip about the town, and it worried him."

"What kind of gossip?" Bennet asked.

"Tell us about this Dutch Ventner first," Jessie suggested. "I've never even heard his name before. Who is he, and why did you and Annie get so nervous when I asked about him?"

Bennet was silent for a moment. Then he said, "It ain't real easy to tell you much about Dutch, Jessie, except that he's maybe the meanest and crookedest man I ever run into."

"I'm mortally afeard of him," Annie broke in. "I didn't want Sid to get mixed up with him any more'n he can help."

"Now, Annie, that's between you and me," Bennet broke in. "It ain't anything that'd interest Jessie and Ki, anyways."

"If they've come all the way from San Francisco to find out about this town of ours, they've got to know about

Dutch," Annie went on, her voice firm. "And I think you'd best tell 'em the whole story, from A to Izzard."

"But, Annie—" Bennet began.

Annie interrupted him almost before he'd started speaking. "I mean the whole story," she went on. "From what all you've told me about Jessie Starbuck and Ki, they ain't going to think none the worse of you after they hear it."

Sid Bennet was silent for a moment. Then he nodded to his wife and said, "Reckon you're right at that, Annie. But there's still coffee in the pot out back, so let's all go set down where we can talk without nobody butting in on us."

"We don't want to put you and Annie to any trouble, Sid," Jessie said.

Before Bennet could reply, Annie answered for him. She said, "It's no trouble, Jessie. We've got plenty of coffee. Sid drinks it like it was water, now that he can't swill redeye the way he used to."

"A cup of coffee would be good right now," Ki put in.

"Of course it would," Jessie agreed. "And if Sid doesn't mind leaving the store unattended—"

"That's what the bell on the door's for," Sid broke in. "I ain't stove up so bad that I can't get in here from the back part to take care of a customer."

Annie had already started for the curtained door at the rear of the store. Jessie and Ki followed her, and Sid fell in behind them.

When Jessie passed through the curtained door she glanced around, taking in her new surroundings with a single sweeping look. The rear of the store had been divided by a partition of unpainted boards into a large room and small one. As Jessie passed the door into the small room she saw that it contained an unmade bed and a battered oak bureau. In the large room a woodburning cookstove radiated a gentle heat. Tiered shelves filled the back wall that stood beyond it. The shelves held stacked dishes, cooking utensils, and a number of burlap bags whose bulging sides gave no hint of their contents.

On the other side of the room there was a round-topped table and a number of chairs. Brackets on the side wall held a rifle, its stock rubbed to the bare wood and carrying the dents and scars of long service. The floor along the back wall was stacked with boxes carrying the burned-in stamp of Arbuckle's Coffee, and several more lumpy burlap bags.

"I guess you can see we're still not settled in," Annie said apologetically as she went to the shelves behind the stove and took down two cups. "There just ain't been time, what with Sid so busy getting the store ready and all."

"We'll get to that later," Sid said. He was settling into the nearest chair as he spoke. Leaning back, he gestured toward the table. "Now, you and Ki set down, Jessie. I can't get around any too good, but I guess you seen that. These gimpy legs of mine don't hold me up too long at a time."

"You must've had an accident of some kind after you left the Circle Star," Jessie frowned. "I don't remember that you had any trouble getting around when you were there."

"I did and I didn't," Sid replied. "I had one knee pretty bad tore up when I got throwed, but it healed all right. Then after I moved down to the Gulf, when Old King Kleberg hired me away from Alex, them Brahma bulls he was having shipped in turned out to be more of a handful than anybody'd figured on. I got stove up real bad down there."

"You got the worst of it there," Annie said as she poured coffee into the cups she'd placed on the table.

"Now, it wasn't nobody's fault but mine, Annie," Sid said quickly. "And Mr. Kleberg done right by me, sending me to that doctor in San Antone. It was what happened afterward that done me in the worst."

"What happened afterward?" Ki asked.

"Oh, I wasn't in no mind to go back down to the King Ranch and tangle with them Brahmas agin," Sid replied. "So I begun to ramble. Picked up a job here and there, not bossing no more, just being as good a hand as I could.

O'course, I got my knees knocked out more'n once, till after a while I wasn't able to make much of a hand for nobody. Things was pretty tight."

"Go on, Sid," Annie said when her husband showed no sign of continuing. "You got to tell Jessie all of it."

"Well, the long and short if it was, I got off of the straight and narrow," Sid went on after a long pause. "Went on the owl-hoot trail."

"You became an outlaw?" Jessie asked, trying to keep the surprise from showing in her voice. "That's the last thing I'd have expected you to do, Sid."

"Well, I'm right ashamed to have to tell you about it, Jessie. And I don't guess I made a very good one. But I robbed a stage or two, and then a bank. That was down in Arizona Territory, and I don't reckon I need to tell you and Ki what their penitentiary was like."

"No," Jessie said when Sid fell silent again. "I've heard about it from several people. They all agree it's the worst of the worst."

"That's where I met up with Dutch Ventner," Sid told her. "And he's about the meanest man I ever run into— mean, but smart, if being an outlaw's smart at all. Anyways, to make a long story short, Dutch had the idee of starting an outlaw town in a place where there wasn't no lawmen welcome."

"Which is what he's done here, I'd guess," Ki put in when Bennet paused.

"That's right, Ki," the old man agreed. "Except it's taken him a long time to get around to it."

"Both of you had to serve out your sentences, I suppose?"

Sid nodded. "Dutch got out first. Him and Annie was both waiting for me in Yuma. I tried to break free, because when me and Annie had our last talk before I was hauled down to Yuma I'd promised her I'd go straight when I got out."

"Dutch did awful things to me," Annie said. Her voice

was little more than a whisper. "I'm still fearful of him."

"Well, the long and the short of it is that I figured the best out I had was to go along with Dutch for a while," Sid told them. "You might say we're serving out our time to him now."

"One thing I don't understand," Ki said when Sid paused. "You and this Dutch Ventner were down close to Mexico when you got out of prison. Why didn't he build his town down along the Mexican border?"

"Oh, he aimed to do just that at first," Sid answered. "But in that part of Mexico the Rurales is thicker'n fleas. And everywhere else, the border's the Rio Grande. It's too big for a man on the run to get across easy, with maybe the Rurales laying for him on the other side."

"So he came up here?" Jessie frowned. "Close to Canada?"

Sid nodded. "That's the idee, Jessie."

"What about the Mounted Police?" Ki asked. "Weren't they after your friend Dutch?"

"They're spread too thin, Ki," Sid replied. "Most of them close to the border is either further east or further west, and there's another big bunch way up in Yukon Territory. The closest one to here's in Moose Jaw, up in Saskatchewan, and that's five hundred miles away."

"Just where is the Canadian border from here, then?" Jessie asked. "It can't be very far."

"Why, I thought you'd tumbled to that before now, Jessie," Sid told her. "The border between the U.S. and Canada runs right smack down the middle of the street. If you step outside of my store and cross the street, you'll be in Canada."

For a moment Jessie and Ki sat in stunned silence, looking at one another. Jessie was the first to speak.

"Then if a lawman caught up with a crook who was wanted on the United States side, all the man would have to do is step across the Canadian boundary, where he couldn't be arrested," Jessie said thoughtfully.

"Or the other way around," Sid agreed.

"I can see how much a crook on the run would like that." Ki frowned. "He could live comfortably in town here, and if a lawman caught up with him, he'd just cross the street."

"That's what Dutch Ventner's counting on," Sid said.

"He's overlooked something, though," Jessie said thoughtfully. "Towns have to have officials, like a mayor and a clerk and councilmen. And the laws aren't the same in this country and Canada, either."

"I hate to tell you this, Jessie," Sid said, "but Dutch has already thought about that. He's figuring on me being the mayor on this side of the border, and some lawyer he run into up at Calgary is going to be the mayor across the line."

"A crooked lawyer, I'd imagine?" Ki asked.

"That's something I can't say. I never laid eyes on the fellow. Dutch is up in Calgary now to get him moved down here."

"And Ventner's already planning on a rigged election on both sides of the international boundary, I'm sure," Jessie frowned.

"Well, I can't answer as to that," Bennet told her. "But I'd be right surprised if he didn't have things all set up."

"There aren't too many people on either side of the border, Jessie," Ki pointed out. "Ventner wouldn't have any trouble keeping control of the votes."

Sid nodded. "That's why he's in such a hurry. The word about this place is still being passed along the outlaw grapevine now, and Dutch says by the time everybody on the owl-hoot trail's heard about it there'll be a lot more that'll come stay here till it's safe for 'em to go back to work again."

"It'll be very profitable for Ventner, I'm sure," Jessie said. "And no risk of him going back to prison. But what about you and Annie?"

"We don't want any part of Ventner or his scheme, Jessie," Sid told her. "But I'm too old and stove-up to buck a man like him, especially with all the help he'd get from the outlaws staying here."

"Does Ventner know you two want to leave?" Ki asked.

"I'm afeared he does, Ki," Sid answered. "Because me and him was old cellmates down in Arizona, I figured if I just up and told him I didn't want to be mayor, and that me and Annie was going to move and live someplace else, he'd be reasonable about it."

"He wasn't, though?" Jessie guessed.

"Not a bit!" Annie put in. "He told Sid that even if me and him did get away, he'd hire some of the men that hides out here to track us down and kill us."

"He'd do it, too," Sid added. "Me and Annie wouldn't have a chance."

"How many wanted men are staying here now?" Jessie asked.

The old man frowned. "I don't rightly know, Jessie. They come and they go, and there ain't no real way for a body to keep count of 'em."

"Make a guess," Ki suggested.

"Well, I'd say forty or fifty at the outside," Sid said thoughtfully. "Some of 'em just comes in and stays a day or two and moves on. But o'course, you got to figure in the ones that's here all the time, like me and Annie and the saloonkeepers and the gamblers that runs the games and the girls in the houses and all like that."

"Sixty or seventy all told, then." Jessie frowned. "And all of them splitting whatever they make with Ventner."

"I'd say that's a fair guess," Sid replied.

"It sounds to me like Ventner's got a very profitable deal going for him here, Jessie," Ki observed. "And it certainly cuts out the risks he'd be taking if he kept robbing banks or trains, or went into cattle rustling."

Jessie nodded. "I'm sure Ventner's thought about that, too. But we've found out what we came here for, Ki. I think the best thing for us to do now is to start back home. We'll tell Congressman Dawson about the situation here.

Then it'll be up to him to decide what he wants to do next."

"Now hold on, Jessie!" Sid Bennet protested. "You can't just up and leave like that! I got a lot of things to ask you about the Circle Star and what all you've been doing, and—" He stopped short as the tinkling of the bell on the store's front door sounded. "Just a minute," he went on. "I got a customer out front. I better go wait on him."

Heaving himself out of his chair with some difficulty, Bennet hobbled to the door and pushed through the curtain. As he disappeared into the store, Jessie turned to Annie.

"Do you think he'll need some help waiting on that customer?" she asked.

Annie shook her head. "Sid likes to do everything he can manage to by hisself, Jessie. Sometimes he gets a mite impatient when I try to help him."

"I can understand that." Jessie replied. She stood up and added, "I'm going to help myself to a little bit more of your coffee, if you don't mind, Annie. It really hits the spot."

"Why, you just help yourself," Annie replied. "There's plenty more where that came from."

Refilling her cup, Jessie turned away from the stove and started back to her chair. She passed the curtain that covered the door, and, hearing the murmur of voices from the front of the store, said, "I'll just peek out and see how Sid's doing."

Pulling aside the curtain, Jessie stepped into the doorway. Bennet was standing behind the counter, talking to one of the two young, travel-stained men in front of it. Both wore the faded blue denim Levi's jeans and flannel shirts favored by ranch hands, and both had holstered revolvers in their gunbelts. The man who had been listening to the conversation between his companion and Bennet caught the motion of the curtain as Jessie pulled it aside. He looked around, stared at her for a moment, then turned back to his companion.

"Hey, Beasley," he said. "Look at what just showed up."

"Well, now!" the second man said. "She's about what I need to fix me up!" Turning back to Bennet, he went on, "You didn't tell us you had a back room here, old man. I figured we'd have to go to a saloon to find us a couple of girls, but this one here's plenty good enough for me!"

"Me too, Pepper," his companion put in. "Unless the old man's got another one just like her in that back room of his."

"Now, wait a minute!" Bennet said. "You're wrong. If you two are looking for women, go on to a saloon or one of the houses. This is just a grocery store!"

"Not with a dame like that around, it ain't!" the man called Beasley said. He started toward Jessie.

"Keep your distance!" Jessie warned him. "In fact, what you two had better do is get out of here right now and ride on into town, where you'll find what you're looking for !"

"Listen to what the lady says!" Bennet told the pair.

"Save your breath, old man!" Pepper said. "I don't know why you're being so damn ornery. We've heard enough about this town to know what's what!"

Both of them had started advancing toward Jessie now. They'd covered perhaps half ther distance down the wide middle aisle when Ki pushed past her.

"From what I heard back there, this is for me to handle," he told her in a half whisper. "Look after Sid; he might need your help."

Jessie looked toward the front of the building. Bennet was moving slowly along the counter, leaning on his canes.

"Don't worry," she said to Ki. "Just get those two rowdies out of here without too much trouble."

By this time the two men were only a short distance from Ki.

"Get outta my way, Chink boy," Pepper warned. When Ki did not move, he raised a fist threateningly.

Ki struck with the speed gained from years of practice.

68

He blocked Pepper's fist with his elbow as his right hand swung in a *tagatana* chop that caught his would-be assailant on the temple. Pepper had time only to let out a surprised grunt before his knees sagged and he fell forward, his jaw slack and his eyes rolling upward.

"You can't do my friend that way!" Beasley grated, lunging forward, his fists swinging.

Ki parried one swinging arm with a *shotei* thrust, ducked below the arc of Beasley's other swinging fist and brought up his free arm, his palm stiffened, to land a *migi-tegatana* strike that sent Beasley to his knees.

Pepper was struggling to his feet by now. Ki locked a hand in the rowdy's gunbelt and swung him around. Bringing up his elbow with a *hiji* strike, he caught Beasley in the jaw with enough force to stun him. Then, grabbing a handful of Beasley's shirt, he hustled the pair to the door and shoved them outside, where they fell sprawling to the ground.

"Do not enter this door again," Ki warned. "Go on to one of the saloons. You will find the kind of women you seek at any of them."

Without waiting for the men to get to their feet, Ki turned back into the store. Jessie had come up to the door to help Sid Bennet. She glanced up at Ki.

"I think we'd better change our plans a bit," she said. "It won't hurt Dawson to wait a few days for word from us. We'd better say here, where Annie and Sid need our help."

Chapter 7

Ki nodded. "Whatever you think is best, Jessie. If we stay awhile, we might also find out some other things that will be of interest to Congressman Dawson."

"I'm sure we will," Jessie agreed. "Besides, if what just happened is a fair example, a town run by the kind of man Dutch Ventner seems to be is an insult to civilization!"

"I'm glad to hear you say that, Jessie," Sid Bennet spoke from the doorway. "Because I've come to feel the same way, and it makes me sorta ashamed to admit I set so much store by what he told me I could look for here."

"Now, there ain't no use crying over milk that's done been spilt," Annie said, peering over her husband's shoulder as she appeared in the doorway. "What we need to do now is to go back and set down and put our heads together and see what we can do to cure things."

"Annie, you know just as good as I do that there ain't going to be nothing changed as long as Dutch is running the town," Sid told his wife as he and Jessie and Ki followed her through the store and back into the kitchen. "And it ain't just Dutch we'd be bucking. Them plug-uglies that's come here to hide out is going to be on his side."

"Perhaps Ki and I can do something, though," Jessie suggested.

"You really mean that, Jessie?" Annie asked hopefully.

"Of course I do!" Jessie assured her.

"How you aim to go about it, Jessie?" Sid asked.

"I don't know yet. But there's bound to be a way, and all we have to do is find it."

"We'll have to find a place to stay, first," Ki pointed out. "I don't imagine that we'd be welcome in the town."

"Even if we could feel safe in any of those places that had signs on them saying 'rooms to rent,' I wouldn't want to stay in one," Jessie went on. "We'd better ride out from town before dark and set up camp away from the land Ventner owns."

"You'd be welcome to stay here with me and Sid," Annie said. Then she frowned and added, "Except that you can see we ain't got no room to spare."

Jessie shook her head. "Thanks, Annie, but I don't want to get you and Sid into trouble. If we were to stay with you, Ventner would give you a share of the blame for anything we did."

Ki turned to Bennet and asked, "How far will we have to go to get off the land Dutch Ventner owns, Sid?"

"Not too far. Dutch's land goes quite a ways in all but one direction," Bennet replied. "I reckon you and Jessie seen that big old house out to the east of town?"

Jessie smiled. "It'd be hard to miss it."

"I took a pretty close look at it," Ki volunteered. "All the shutters are closed and there aren't any signs it's being lived in."

"It ain't, Ki," Sid said. "And it ain't on Dutch's land, either. It still belongs to the folks that built it. Ransom is their name, but that ain't important. The thing is, they kept the house and the land it sets on for fifty yards all the way around it. Dutch's property line ends just this side of it and goes on beyond it."

"Why on earth didn't he buy the house when he was getting together the land the town's on?" Jessie asked.

"He didn't on account of he couldn't," Sid replied. "And he's real mad about not being able to get his hands on it."

"What stopped him?" Jessie asked. "Except for the house, he seems to have made a pretty clean sweep."

Sid nodded. "That's what he set out to do. But the way I heard it, that Ransom family used to own just about all the land on both sides of the border hereabouts. Dutch tried to buy everything they had when he set out to build the town, but they wouldn't sell the old family home or the land it sets on."

"It's just a deserted house, then?" Jessie asked.

"There ain't none of the family living in it, if that's what you mean," Sam replied. "I hear they moved back East, to Winnipeg or someplace. But it still belongs to them."

"As long as it doesn't belong to Ventner, I don't suppose he could keep us from camping by the house, then," Jessie said thoughtfully. "Ki, that looks like our best bet. Where there's a house like that, I'm sure there'll be a well."

"There is," Sam told her. "Out back of the place, where the barns and bunkhouse used to be."

"I wondered why the house was all by itself out there," Jessie said. "It looks odd, sort of lonesome."

"I guess it was a lot different before Dutch took over here," Sid told her.

"I can understand how those people must have felt," Jessie said. "Even if they didn't intend to live in it again, it's still their family home."

"I guess so." Sid nodded. "Anyhow, Dutch took the barns and the bunkhouse that was back of it. He moved the

73

barns up here and turned 'em into saloons. This store building I rent from him used to be part of the bunkhouse. He used the rest of the lumber out of it to build some of the shanties he rents out."

"No wonder the house looks odd, standing all by itself," Jessie observed. "But as long as it isn't on Ventner's land, I don't suppose he'll be able to bother us."

"Oh, soon as Dutch finds out about you and Ki being here, he'll try to bluff you into leaving," Annie said. "Just don't pay him no mind."

"Don't worry, Annie," Jessie promised. "Ki and I can take care of ourselves." She turned to Ki and went on, "Let's ride out and look at the place, Ki. It's not far. Then we can come back and get whatever supplies we'll need from Sid."

Ki picked up a stone and tapped the iron pipe that protruded a foot or more above the ground. He listened to the dull, muted chiming noise that resulted, then stood up and nodded to Jessie.

"There's water in this pipe," he told her. "We have all we'll need for tonight, and I'll borrow a wrench from Sid tomorrow to take the cap off. Then we won't have to depend on getting water from the town."

"And as long as this good weather holds, we won't have to worry about putting up a tent or even a fly," Jessie said. "I guess we can go ahead and set our camp up, Ki."

"I'm satisfied if you are, Jessie," Ki said. "We've camped in a lot worse places."

"And if it rains, we'll just take Sid and Annie up on their invitation to run down to their store," Jessie went on. "But at this time of year, I don't think we need to worry about getting any storms."

After their quick preliminary look at the deserted house, Jessie and Ki had ridden back to Bennet's store and replenished their dwindling stock of provisions. Annie had insisted that they stay for supper, and they'd had an early

74

meal. They'd cut their visit short in order to return to the deserted house and set up their camp before darkness fell.

Seen at close hand during their earlier ride around it, the house had proved to be even more imposing than it had been when viewed from a distance. It was a large dwelling, two stories high, built of lumber set on a foundation of mortared stone blocks, and it was obvious at a glance that the big place had been well cared for. Its paint was still shining, the pine shakes that covered its slanting roof showed no signs of curling or warping, and all the windows were tightly closed with board shutters. When Ki and Jessie tried the doors they found that those at both front and back were locked.

Around the house itself, traces of the barn and other buildings that had flanked it were clearly visible. It was apparent that the house had not been vacant long enough for the natural vegetation to intrude on the ground surrounding it. The short mountain grass had not yet grown thick enough to cover the places where the bunkhouse and barns and privies had stood.

Very little imagination had been required to give Jessie and Ki a good idea of how the place must have looked when it had still been occupied by its original builders.

Now Jessie went on, "We shouldn't be here more than a few days. Just long enough to find out all the details we can of what that Dutch Ventner's up to."

"We've got a pretty good idea by now of the scheme he's hatched up," Ki said. "But it seems to me that both the U.S. and Canada are going to have to work together to end it, since it overlaps into both countries."

"That's something Congressman Dawson will have to figure out. Of course, he's in the right place to do it."

Ki had walked a few paces away from the spot where they'd chosen to spread their bedrolls, close to the wall of the house on the side opposite the town. He stood for a moment looking out over the little shallow vale that sloped away from the dwelling. Then he turned back to Jessie.

"We'd better tether our horses tonight, Jessie," he said. "Some strays from town seem to have wandered out here while we were gone."

"They probably belong to one of the outlaws who's just come here to hole up," Jessie answered. "Come to think of it, I didn't notice a livery stable in town. But there's plenty of grass for two or three horses besides ours, Ki."

"Suppose the crook who put them to graze is a horse thief?" Ki asked.

"That hadn't occurred to me. You're right. I'm sure there are plenty of horse thieves in that town. We'll play safe and put ours on a tether close to our bedrolls."

"I'm just about ready to crawl into mine," Ki said. "I'll tie the horses to the well standpipe before I do, though. It's close enough for us to hear anybody who comes prowling."

"That'll be fine," Jessie agreed. "And even if it's not quite dark yet, I'm ready to go to bed, too. We can make our plans tomorrow morning while we eat breakfast."

Jessie could not be sure whether a noise had awakened her or whether she'd been roused from a sound sleep by the thin thread of light that was now shining across her face from a slit between the shutters of the house. She lay completely motionless while she blinked her eyes. They'd begun to water, and her pupils were still widely dilated by sleep and darkness. She moved her head a few inches to avoid the thread-thin beam.

In the night's moonless dark, the line of light shone like a beacon. Though the slit between the shutters of the upstairs window from which it came was only the smallest fraction of an inch wide, little more than a hairline, the ray cast a widening strip of brightness across Jessie's face and beyond it along the thinly-grassed ground before the gloom of night swallowed it.

Wiping the moisture from her eyes, Jessie sat up in her blankets, shrugging them aside. The chill of the thin night air in the high altitude struck her skin and she reached for her blouse and shrugged into it. A short distance away she saw the oblong lump of Ki's bedroll. It was close enough to hers to allow her to hear the soft susurrus of Ki's breathing in the silent night.

"Ki!" Jessie whispered. She pitched her voice low, the faintest whisper, but Ki woke instantly.

"What's wrong, Jessie?" he whispered. His voice was as soft as hers, a bare breath that would have been inaudible three or four yards away.

"That window, Ki," Jessie breathed. "Look at the light coming from it."

"I noticed it when I opened my eyes," Ki told her. "Did you hear a noise, or was it just the light that woke you up?"

"Just the light, I'm sure. I think I'd remember if there was a noise as well."

"Somebody must be in the house, then," Ki said. His voice was thoughtful. "We'd certainly have noticed that window if there's been light coming from it before we went to bed."

"Of course we would. And we'd have heard anybody prowling around, or opening a door. Do you think there's been somebody inside all the time?" Jessie asked.

"I don't see how there could've been. As quiet as it is out here away from town, we'd have been sure to hear them as they moved around."

"We'd better do a little investigating," Jessie said decisively. "I can't understand this any better than you do, but we'll have to find out who's in there."

As Jessie spoke she was slipping into her tight-fitting riding jeans. She pushed her feet into her boots and slid her arms into the sleeves of the blouse she'd draped around her shoulders when she first awakened. A few feet away she could hear the rustling of Ki's clothing as he, too, dressed.

Both Jessie and Ki had used their blanket-draped saddles as pillows. Jessie slid her hand under the edge of the blanket that covered her saddle and closed her fingers around her Colt. She could see Ki standing up now, a faint

77

ghostly figure in the moonless night.

"I'm ready if you are," she said.

"Anytime," Ki told her, stepping away from his bedroll. "We'd better circle the house before we do anything else, to see if there are signs of how many might be inside."

"Yes," Jessie agreed. "But what I can't understand is how even a mouse could get in there without us hearing it."

"I'd think so, too. Whoever it is, they'd have had to've ridden out here from town, or turned off the road. And they must've come on foot. We'd certainly have heard horses if they'd been riding."

"That's what I can't understand," Jessie said. "We're a good quarter of a mile from the road, and there's not a horse alive able to move that far without making a single sound."

"Well, we'll find out soon enough," Ki told her. He was at Jessie's side now, and matched her steps as she moved cautiously toward the front of the big house.

"We'll stay close together," she said as they started. "If there's somebody inside—and there's bound to be—there might be somebody else prowling around outside."

"I was about to say the same thing, even though I don't see how somebody could be anywhere around here without at least one of us hearing them."

They'd reached the front corner of the house now, and as though acting on a prearranged signal, both Jessie and Ki looked back along the side they'd just traversed. No signs of light showed from any of the blinds except the one that still bore the thin, bright line which had awakened them. Rounding the corner of the house, they glanced at its facade. No lights showed, the shutters at all the windows were closed.

"I'll step up on the porch and try the door," Ki whispered to Jessie. "My sandals will make less noise than your boots."

"Go ahead," she told him. "I'll cover you, even though

78

it doesn't seem necessary. There doesn't appear to be anybody around here."

Ki stepped soundlessly up the steps leading to the wide veranda, crossed it, and cautiously tried the front door. It was locked.

Moving on, Jessie and Ki stopped silently along the front of the house to the corner and looked along the side they had not yet explored. All the shutters were closed as tightly as the other had been, and none of them showed a gleam of brightness.

There were no glints of light showing from the shuttered windows of the side opposite that from which they'd spread their blankets. They moved along it, their ears straining to hear any alien nose, but the darkness stayed silent. At the rear corner, the darkness was equally dense, and unbroken by light. The shed-roof of the abbreviated rear porch cast the back door into a deeper shadow than they'd yet encountered, and they started along it toward the steps.

"I'd better try the back door," Ki whispered.

"Chances are it'll be locked as tightly as the front door was," Jessie said. "But you'd better go ahead and find out."

Ki went up the steps to the porch, his sandals whispering as he mounted them. Two steps led him to the door and he turned the knob and tried to open it. To his surprise, the door yielded. Ki did not open it at once. He pulled the door closed again as softly as he'd opened it, but when he released the doorknob the catch grated, a tiny sound, but one that seemed very loud in the night's quiet.

"Jessie!" he whispered. "Wasn't this door locked when we tried it this afternoon on our first trip out here?"

"Of course it was," she said. "If it had been open, we'd remember."

"It's open now," he told her. "Be ready to cover me. I'm going inside."

"Go ahead," Jessie whispered. "I'm ready."

Ki turned the doorknob again. He took a half step backward and shifted his body to one side, then with a sudden swift move pushed hard against the door. It swung halfway open, then stopped with the loud thunk of hard wood meeting metal.

A rifle in the darkened room barked. Its muzzle blast, red in the darkness, gave Jessie and Ki a fleeting glimpse of a human figure brought into sharp relief by the blinding flash before the brief glare died and the darkness became total again.

★

Chapter 8

Blinded by the muzzle blast of the shot fired from the door, Jessie triggered off an unaimed shot from her Colt. She heard the slug crash through the door with a splintering of hard wood.

Beside her, Ki slid a *shuriken* blade from his wrist-case into his hand, and stepped out of the line of fire from inside the house. He stood poised, ready to launch the razor-edged throwing blade at anyone who came through the dark doorway.

As he moved, Ki called, "Drop flat, Jessie!"

Jessie had been standing with her Colt ready, but Ki's command reminded her of her vulnerability, and she dropped to the porch floor. She lifted the muzzle of her revolver to cover the door. Her vision had cleared now, and she could see the door's opening as a black rectangle against the lesser darkness that shrouded the porch.

Surprisingly, the rifle did not bark again. Instead of its loud report they heard a woman's voice.

"You can sit up," she said, "Just don't lift your guns or make any sudden moves. Remember, I can see you against the sky, even if it's dark, and I'm ready to pull the trigger if you do."

"Don't worry," Jessie replied. "We don't intend to shoot. Or to move, either. But we don't even know who you are or what you're doing here."

"I could say the same thing about you," the woman answered. "And I don't mind telling you who I am. I'm Monica Ransom, and I happen to own this house."

"My name's Jessica Starbuck," Jessie called back in reply. "And if your name's Ransom, I already know this house belongs to you—or to your family."

"Anybody who's been around this part of the country for a day or even less could know that," the woman said. "Now tell me who the man with you is."

"His name is Ki," Jessie responded unhesitatingly. Now that the woman in the house had identified herself, the keen edge of tension on which she'd been poised was easing. She went on, "Ki is—well, it's a bit hard to explain to somebody I'm telling for the first time. Ki was my father's good right hand for many years and now he helps me just as he did my father."

"That still doesn't explain what you're doing here," Monica Ransom reminded Jessie.

"Congressman Dawson asked us to come here and find out what's going on in the town yonder."

"I'm acquainted with the congressman myself," Monica Ransom said. She was silent for a moment, then went on, "It's easy to mention names, I've found. I suppose you can prove what you've just told me?"

"There are some papers in my saddlebag," Jessie answered. "But no letters or anything from Congressman Dawson, if that's what it'll take to convince you. All I have is a few letters adressed to me at my ranch in Texas, business letters, things like that. I don't know whether you'd call them proof of anything except that I have them."

"We're a long way from Texas," the other woman said. "And you're right, you could show me any number of letters and I still wouldn't know whether or not you were proving who you are."

"I'm afraid that's the best I can do," Jessie replied. "I don't have a passport with me and neither does Ki, because we didn't plan to leave the United States."

"Tell me why you came here," Monica Dawson suggested.

"I've already told you that," Jessie protested.

"Tell me again," Monica insisted. "Why should a congressman ask you to make any sort of investigation? Why didn't he send one of the men from the Secret Service?"

"Perhaps because he didn't want to stir up things with an official investigation," Jessie replied. "Ki and I ran into him quite by accident at the Palace Hotel in San Francisco. The congressman and my father were friends. In fact, it was Alex who persuaded him to run for office the first time. But I don't suppose my telling you all this proves anything, either."

"It may not prove anything, but the way you've talked to me certainly does," Monica said. Doubt no longer tinged her voice.

"You believe me, then?" Jessie asked.

"Strangely enough, I do," Monica answered. "I'm familiar with the Starbuck name, of course. I don't suppose there are many people in the United States or Canada who haven't heard it. And the way you answered me, not trying to force me to reach a conclusion—Well, Jessica Starbuck, I think I've had enough experience to recognize the truth when I hear it. You and your friend come inside while I light the lamp."

By the time Jessie and Ki got inside the house, Monica had touched a match to the wick of a coal-oil lamp that stood on the kitchen table. Blinking as their eyes adjusted to the light, they studied their impromptu hostess while she pulled chairs up to the kitchen table. The rifle she'd fired lay across the table. It was an old octagonal-barreled Hotchkiss.

Monica Dawson looked to be in her early thirties. She was a tall woman, angular in her features, a dark-eyed brunette who in an era of long hair wore hers cropped into a shoulder length bob. Her chin was pointed, her cheekbones high, and her nose sharp and prominent, with flaring nostrils. The one feature of her face that seemed incongruous was her mouth. It was a bit over-generous, with full lips that seemed to be perpetually pouting. She wore a loose cambric blouse tucked into a riding-skirt. Her feet were bare.

While Jessie was taking stock of Monica Dawson, the other woman was subjecting Jessie and Ki to her scrutiny. At last the small frown on her face cleared away and she nodded.

"You gave me a very rude surprise," she told Jessie. "I didn't see anyone around when I rode in late this afternoon, so I unloaded by pack horse and started getting settled down for the night."

"Then those were your horses that we saw grazing close to the house when we got back from town," Jessie said.

Monica nodded. "They must've been. I was really tired after my long ride, so I lay down in one of the upstairs bedrooms to nap a few minutes. It was pitch dark when I woke up, and I didn't know how long I'd been sleeping. I lighted a lamp, but of course none of the clocks were working, because they hadn't been wound up for a long time. None of the family's been back here since we moved to Medicine Hat."

"It must've been a shock for you to find that Ki and I had taken over the back of your house for our camp, then," Jessie smiled.

"Of course it was!" Monica agreed. "There hadn't been a sign of anybody coming onto the place when I got here. As I said, I was tired after being in the saddle all day. I didn't do much except glance around. Then I came inside to rest. It was so restful that I fell asleep, which I certainly didn't intend to do."

"I'm sorry we surprised you," Jessie said. "But you surprised us about as much as we did you. When we turned in, the house was dark and silent. We saw your horses, but thought they belonged to somebody in town who'd put them out here to graze."

"When I looked out the window and saw your horses and then your bedrolls, I just jumped to the conclusion that you were a couple of outlaws who'd just come to town," Monica went on. "I came downstairs and got my father's old rifle and—Well, all of us know the rest."

"Ki and I just got here today ourselves," Jessie said. "We took a quick look at the town—what there is of it— and decided we'd be better off camping out than going into one of those disreputable rooming houses. One of our old friends—a man who used to be my father's foreman on our ranch in Texas—is running a store in town. He suggested that we come out here to camp for the night because your house is on the only land around here that Dutch Ventner doesn't own."

"You've met Ventner, then?" Monica asked.

Jessie shook her head. "We've heard of him, but neither Ki nor I have ever seen him."

"Believe me, you don't want to!" Monica exclaimed. "I met him when he was buying land from us. I don't know whether you've found this out yet, but my family owned most of the land that Ventner's built his town on."

"That was one of the first things we learned," Ki nodded.

Jessie broke in to ask, "I suppose you've just come to look around and see what's happening to your old home?"

"Partly that," Monica said, and nodded. "But Father wanted me to get some papers that he'd left in his old desk when we moved. He's in no condition to do any travelling, so I volunteered. Of course, I was as curious to see what was happening here as you must've been."

"As I told you a minute ago, it was Congressman Dawson who persuaded Ki and me to come here," Jessie replied. "He'd heard rumors of this outlaw town that Ventner's building."

"You've found out enough to convince you the stories that he plans to use the town as an outlaw's haven are true?" Monica frowned.

Jessie nodded. "There's no doubt about it. Ventner doesn't even seem to be trying to keep it a secret."

"That's going to make my father very unhappy." Monica frowned. "When he first heard rumors of what's going on, I had a terrible time keeping him from coming here with me. He was sure that all he'd have to do would be to go to Ventner and tell him we wanted to buy back our land and Ventner would sell it to us."

"I don't think he'd have had much luck, even if he'd come back," Ki said. "From what our friends here tell us, Ventner's gone too far with his plans to change anything."

Monica nodded. "I tried to tell Father that. But he's so used to having his own way that I couldn't convince him it'd be a waste of time."

"What are you planning to do then, now that you're here?" Jessie asked.

"I really don't know," Monica confessed. "On the way from Medicine Hat I tried to think of an argument that would persuade Ventner to sell, but everything I thought of just seemed silly."

"I doubt that you'll have any luck," Jessie said. "From what our friends told us, this Ventner's a dyed-in-the-wool hard case."

Monica nodded. "He is. I only saw him once or twice when father was negotiating the sale of our property, but I thought he was a very repulsive individual."

"I've never seen Dutch Ventner," Jessie said. "But from what I've heard about him, I'm prepared to dislike him."

"You won't be making a mistake," Monica assured her. "And if you have any ideas about how I can get back the land we sold him and satisfy my father, I'm certainly ready to listen."

"I can think of only one thing," Jessie said, frowning thoughtfully.

"Tell me," Monica invited.

"Ki and I have an old friend here," Jessie went on. "He used to be the foreman of the Circle Star, the ranch my father owned in Texas. He's— Well, you might as well know the facts right at the beginning. Sid Bennet, the man I'm talking about, got into some trouble after he left the Circle Star and served a term in prison down in Arizona. He and Ventner were in the same cell. If anybody in this place knows the way Ventner's mind works, it'd be Sid."

"An ex-convict?" Monica frowned. "Do you think you could trust him?"

"Of course, or I wouldn't have mentioned him," Jessie said. "But it's getting late—or early, if it's past midnight —and I suggest we go back to sleep and talk about this tomorrow."

"I'll add something to your suggestion, Jessie," Monica said quickly. "Bring your bedding in the house where you can have a real bed instead of sleeping on the ground."

"Are you sure you—"

"I never make an offer I'm not sure about," Monica broke in. "There's all the space in the world here, and I don't see any reason to waste it."

"I don't mind telling you, the idea of sleeping in a bed appeals to me right now," Jessie told her. "Since Ki and I left the train at Spokane we've been camping out at night, and it'll be a real treat to sleep indoors in a bed."

Jessie and Ki went outside and began gathering up their bedrolls. As they started back toward the kitchen door, Jessie said, "I think we've got a real ally in Monica Ransom, Ki. Now if Sid and Annie can give us a lead on what Ventner's been up to lately, we've got somebody on our side that the authorities on both sides of the border will listen to."

87

"You're thinking about turning him over to the law, I suppose?" Ki asked.

"Of course. If he's in prison, that'd be the end of this outlaw hideout he's getting organized up here."

"Putting Ventner behind bars would solve the problem," Ki agreed. "Without him leading the outlaws, his whole scheme would just wither away and die."

"We'll sleep on it," Jessie said. "All three of us need to rest until morning. Then we'll see how the idea looks to us in broad daylight."

"I think your idea's a good one, Jessie," Monica Ransom said thoughtfully as they sat around the breakfast table the following morning. "Ventner's the key, all right. If he goes to prison, there'd be nobody to carry on with his plans."

"Then let's ride into town and talk to Sid and Annie," Jessie suggested. "And see if we can get some sort of idea what Ventner's been up to lately."

"There'd still be the problem of finding somebody to arrest him and put him in prison," Monica said.

"Yes, that's the only weak spot in our idea," Ki agreed. "You know the country better than Jessie and I do, Monica. Is there a sheriff's office or a United States Marshal's office anywhere close by?"

Monica shook her head. "No. The nearest one's at Spokane. But there's an outpost of the Royal Northwest Mounted Police at Fort McLeod, and that's only a two-day ride from here."

"Then one of us can go after him, if we find out that Ventner's wanted in Canada," Jessie said. "It'd certainly be easier than going all the way back to Spokane."

Ki broke into the conversation between Jessie and Monica. His voice was diffident as he suggested, "Before we start planning who's going to arrest Ventner, shouldn't we find out if we can come up with a reason for them to arrest him?"

"Ki's right, you know." Jessie smiled at Monica. "We'd better go have our talk with Sid and Annie."

"Oh, Dutch ain't a bit bashful when it comes to talking about the things he's done," Sid Bennet told Jessie after she'd explained their plan. "And he's been into a lot of mighty bad crooked deals."

"Then we ought to be able to have him arrested," Jessie said. "Preferably for something that will keep him in prison for several years."

Bennet frowned and went on. "Trouble is, Dutch don't talk to anybody that ain't as mean and crooked as he is. The kind of folks he talks to about the things he's done, the jobs he's pulled and all, they ain't going to testify in court. They're on the wrong side of the law, too."

"How about you or Annie?" Jessie asked. "Both of you must know about some of the crimes he's committed."

"We've sure heard plenty of his talk," Bennet replied. "But I don't see no way we could prove nothing against him. It'd just be his word against ours."

"Maybe Bella could help us," Annie said suddenly. "She's always telling me how mad she is at Dutch for the way he treated her after she stood lookout on all of them bank holdup jobs him and Spud Peters pulled up in Calgary."

"Who is Bella?" Monica asked.

"She's working the floor at the Sunset Saloon right now," Annie replied. "Which is a sorta come-down after her being Dutch's girl for such a long time."

"You and this girl are friends, then?" Monica asked.

Annie nodded. "About as much as anybody in this place, I guess. There ain't much chance for folks to get acquainted easy, living in the kind of town where just about everybody's here today and gone tomorrow."

"You think she'd testify against him?" Bennet frowned.

"All I can do is ask her," Annie replied. "She comes in

here now and again, and we've sorta got in the habit of visiting together for a few minutes after I fill her order."

"Has she been in lately?" Jessie asked.

"No. She didn't come in yesterday or so far today," Annie replied. "Which means she oughta be coming in today or tomorrow."

"Ask her, then," Jessie suggested. "And if she says she'll testify, Ki and Monica and I will meet with her and explain what we want her to do."

"You might tell her that we'll do something nice for her if she helps us out," Monica said. "Not that we're trying to bribe her or anything like that, but perhaps I could find a nice job for her in Medicine Hat, if she'd like to get out of the kind of life she must be leading."

"I'm sure that if you can't find some kind of work for her, I could," Jessie put in. "Or Congressman Dawson could. But be sure to suggest that if she helps us get rid of Ventner, we'll see that she's taken care of."

"I'll keep it in mind next time I see her," Annie promised. "And I'll tell her—"

Annie was interrupted by the tinkle of the bell that hung on the front door. She turned to look, and after a quick glance turned back to the others with a smile. "Talk about the devil," she said. "That's Bella coming in the door right now."

Bella was a large woman. She was not fat, but she was of the statuesque type that draws instant attention, whether in a frontier village or a large city. Her movements as she entered the store were those of a young woman, but her face was deeply lined and haggard. Her hair was hennaed, her cheeks layered with rouge and powder, and her full lips heavily rouged. The contrast between her face and the plain gingham house dress she had on was so marked as to be almost startling.

"Oh my!" she exclaimed. Her voice was raspy. "I didn't look for you to be so busy, Annie. Listen, honey, I'll just go do some of the little errands I got to take care of, then

I'll come back when you ain't so busy."

"No, no!" Annie said. "Come on in, Bella. These folks aren't customers, just some friends of mine and Sid's. As a matter of fact, I'd just mentioned you to them."

"Me?" Bella frowned, her eyes widening. "Why, what'd you have to say about me to a bunch of strangers?"

"Nothing bad, you can be sure of that," Annie assured her. "But let me introduce you to them."

"Why—I don't think—" Bella began, but Annie had her by the arm now. She introduced her to Jessie, Ki, and Monica.

When the introductions were completed the group stood in silence, the awkward silence when strangers of widely disparate types were gauging one another, trying to come up with some kind of casual comment.

Jessie broke the silence. "Annie was just saying you and Dutch Ventner used to be close friends."

"I—I know Dutch, sure," Bella replied. The pitch of her voice made her reply a question rather than an answer. She went on, "But I don't see what that's got to do with anything."

"We'd like to talk with you about some of the—" Monica began, but stopped short for a moment, searching for the right words to use. She went on, "about some of the things Ventner did when you were with him."

Bella stared at Monica for a moment, her eyes widening. Then she turned to Annie and burst out, "You been talking about me behind my back, Annie! And here I figured you to be about the closest thing to a friend I had! You know I didn't look for you to say nothing to nobody else about me and Dutch! And I won't! There ain't nobody going to turn me into a stool pigeon!"

Turning, Bella stamped out of the store, leaving the others staring at the closing door.

Chapter 9

"Well, I never did see Bella act that way before," Annie said as she stared at the closed door.

"Maybe she's not as mad at Dutch as you figured she was," Sid suggested.

"Or maybe she was too embarrassed to talk, with all of us strangers listening," Ki added.

"It could be part of both," Annie agreed. She turned to Jessie and went on, "I'm sorry as all get-out, Jessie. I was certain that Bella would jump at a chance to get even with Dutch, but it looks like I was wrong."

"No harm's been done," Annie," Jessie assured her. "All we'll have to do is look around for somebody else who can tell us what we're after."

"But do try to think of someone else who might be inclined to help us," Monica told Annie. "There must be somebody else in this town who's angry with Ventner."

"That's the best idea," Jessie seconded. "I'm sure you'll

remember someone around here besides Bella who has a grudge to settle with him."

"Well, I sure got one I'd like to put paid to," Sid volunteered. "Him getting me and Annie to pull up the little roots we'd begun to put down and come out here. Dutch made us an awful lot of promises that he ain't showed no signs of keeping."

"Then put your mind to remembering names," Jessie suggested. "It doesn't really matter who we get to tell us about Ventner. The important thing is to find somebody who has the information we need, and who's willing to pass it on to us."

"In the meantime, we'd better get some supplies and go back out to the house," Ki broke in to suggest. "Breakfast was pretty skimpy, and by the time we get back there and get something cooked up, we'll all be ready for a real meal."

Signs that the day was coming to a close were showing in the western sky. Jessie, Ki, and Monica were sitting in the parlor, chatting idly, getting better acquainted, when Ki glanced out the window.

"We're about to have company," he announced. "It's the woman we tried to get to talk to us this morning at Sid's store."

"Bella?" Jessie frowned, turning to the window to look past Ki at the approaching rider. Turning back to the others, she went on, "There's only one reason I can think of why she'd be coming out here."

"She's changed her mind," Monica said quickly.

"Exactly," Jessie nodded.

"When we asked her to tell us about her life with Dutch Ventner, we may have stirred up memories of the times when he didn't treat her any too well," Monica went on.

"That's what I was thinking," Ki said. He started toward the door. "I'll go out and be there when she pulls up, and tell her I'll take care of her horse. I'll stay outside. She

94

might talk more freely if only the two of you are there listening."

"A good idea," Jessie agreed. "Having so many people at the store to hear her talk about Ventner might have been one reason she left so quickly this morning."

Ki was waiting beside the porch when Bella reined in. As he stepped forward, he extended his arm and said, "Jessie and Monica are waiting for you inside. We saw you riding up."

"I guess you figured out that I changed my mind after I had a chance to think about what Miz Ransom wanted me to do this morning," she said after she'd dismounted.

"It's a lady's privilege to do that," Ki smiled. "Jessie and Monica are inside. I know they'd like to talk to you alone, so I'll stay out here."

With a nod, Bella went into the house. Ki led the horse to the well standpipe and looped the reins around it, then strolled away around the side of the house, where he sat down on the veranda and studied the ramshackle town.

Inside, neither Jessie nor Monica had made any reference to the scene in the store that morning. They did not ask Bella any questions, but invited her to sit at the table with them and have a cup of coffee. Bella said little besides "thank you" when they invited her to sit down and when Monica filled her coffee cup. She studied them with a small puzzled frown on her face as she looked from one of them to the other.

"I changed my mind," she said at last. "But I guess you knew that when you seen me riding up."

Jessie nodded. "We thought you might have."

"I know a little bit about you, Miz Starbuck," Bella went on. "I bet I've heard Sid say something about you or your daddy a hundred times," Bella went on. "And I guess it was them that given you the idea I might know something about Dutch that you'd be interested in hearing."

"You've talked to them since we met you at the store this morning?" Jessie asked.

Bella nodded. "After I got back to my room, I set down and thought about things a lot. About me and Dutch, I mean. And about Sid and Annie, too. And your folks, too, Miz Ransom. Of course, I heard a lot about you and them. Me and Dutch was still—still keeping company then, when he was dickering to buy their land."

"You were still—friends, then?" Monica asked.

"Oh, sure. Me and Dutch goes back a long ways," Bella said. The discomfort or embarrassment that had been so obvious when she first came in was reflected in her voice as she went on, "I guess Sid's told you that, though."

"He did mention it," Jessie replied. "And he said you'd know more about Ventner than anyone else he could think of."

"Why're you so interested in Dutch, Miz Starbuck?" Bella asked with a puzzled frown. "I can see why Miz Ransom is, on account of her folks living here on this place so long, but Sid said you live way off down in Texas."

Jessie hesitated for a moment as she sought the best way to answer Bella's unexpected questions without giving too much away. Finally she said, "A very good friend of my family asked Ki and me to come up here and find out what was going on. Anything that happens in Idaho Territory interests him a great deal."

"I see," Bella nodded. "And it was him that asked you and your Chinaman friend to come up here?"

"Yes," Jessie nodded. "And by the way, Ki isn't Chinese, he's Japanese. He was with my father for many years, and after Alex's—my father's—death, he stayed on with me."

"So that's the way of it." Bella nodded. "I guess everybody in town's been wondering about you and him since you rode in yesterday."

Monica Ransom had been growing increasingly impatient during the long conversation between Bella and Jessie. Now she said, "I hope you came out here to answer some of the questions we wanted to ask this morning?"

"Well, I sorta had that in mind, Miz Ransom," Bella said. Turning to Jessie, she explained, "I went back to the store and had a talk with Annie and Sid after I turned you down this morning. They told me a little bit about how long they'd known you and all that. I knew about Miz Ransom, see, but I never had heard about you before."

"I'm afraid we were trying to rush you into helping us without explaining why," Jessie apologized. "But finding out about Ventner's criminal activities would be worth a great deal to Monica and me. When you were with him, I understand that you helped him by acting as lookout for him on some bank robberies. Is that true?"

Bella nodded. "Oh, sure, I was crazy mad about Dutch then."

"And because you were forced to be apart a lot, didn't you write him letters?"

"Sure. He even answered 'em most of the time, especially when he was planning a job."

"Did he write about his plans for those jobs?"

"Most of the time. I had to know what I'd be having to do, you know."

"Then we'd certainly like to see those, in particular," Jessie said.

"I ain't real proud of all that, you know, Miz Starbuck," Bella said. "And I still ain't real sure I oughta let you see 'em, even with things the way they are now between me and Dutch."

"Between Monica and her family and my own friends, I'm sure we could arrange things so that you wouldn't be punished for what you did in the past," Jessie said.

"You'd be on the side of the law this time," Monica added quickly. "And Jessie's right. Between us we have enough friends in high places to see that you wouldn't suffer."

"Well—" Bella said, her face knitted into a worried frown, "I'd need to be right sure."

"You can be sure," Jessie assured her. "And it'd be

worth a substantial reward from the authorities, I'm positive. That would be in addition to any reward we'd give you privately."

"Well, seeing as how I could use some money to get outta this place and settle down, I guess I'd be interested in making a deal with you and Miz Ransom, then," Bella said. "There's a lot in 'em about the jobs Dutch was planning, and—well, they go back quite a ways."

"I hope you brought the letters with you," Jessie went on, hiding her interest by keeping her voice casual.

"As a matter of fact, I didn't. There ain't much room for me to store a lot of truck in the room I got at the Sunset. That room's for my business, if you gather my meaning."

"Yes," Jessie nodded. "Where are they, then?"

"I rent a little shanty over on the far side of town to live in," Bella answered. "All my own stuff's there, the letters and things like that."

"Then you're going to give us a look at the letters you got from Dutch Ventner?" Monica asked.

"Well, some of 'em wouldn't be much account to you, if getting the goods on Dutch is what you're after. But there's some that Dutch wrote me when he was setting up a job. Ain't that what you're looking for?"

"Exactly," Monica said quickly.

"Yes, indeed," Jessie said at almost the same time.

Both Monica and Jessie stopped short and looked at one another, smiling. Then Monica went on, "You've had a lot more experience than I have with things of this sort, Jessie. Why don't you talk for both of us and save confusion?"

Jessie nodded. "Of course, if that's what you want me to do." She turned back to Bella and asked, "If you didn't bring the letters with you, when can we get a look at them?"

"Why, whenever it suits you," Bella answered.

"Could you bring them out here for us to examine?" Jessie asked.

"I guess maybe I could," Bella said slowly, her brows

drawn together. "But it'd waste a lot of time, me going in and coming way back out here with the letters and waiting while you looked at 'em. I got to be at the Sunset before the evening rush starts up. Seems like to me it'd be easier if one of you ladies was to go to my other place with me."

"Of course it would," Monica said briskly. She turned to Jessie and went on, "I don't mind going, Jessie, but you've had a lot more experience than I have in things of this kind. Why don't you go with Bella and look over the letters?"

"I'll be glad to, of course," Jessie nodded. "We can—"

"Just a minute, now," Bella broke in. "We ain't talked yet about how much it's going to be worth to you to look at them letters."

"Suppose you tell us what you think would be a fair price," Jessie suggested.

"Well, I ain't done any figuring, yet," Bella frowned. "All I know is that a girl situated like I am has got to look out for herself in a place like this."

"Of course you do." Jessie said. "Suppose we say fifty dollars?"

Bella shook her head. Her voice very sober, she said, "If Dutch was to get wind of this, my life wouldn't be worth a plugged nickel, Miz Starbuck. Fifty ain't near enough."

Monica broke in quickly. "I can see Bella's point, Jessie. Suppose we each put up fifty dollars."

"That would be all right," Jessie nodded. Then, turning back to Bella, she asked, "Does that sound fair to you?"

"It sounds a lot better'n fifty."

"Remember," Jessie reminded her, "We're taking the chance there'll be something in the letters that will send Dutch Ventner to prison."

"Don't worry about that, Miz Starbuck," Bella replied. "I was with Dutch on a lot of jobs, and he sent me letters about most of 'em."

"Then we agree on a hundred dollars?" Jessie persisted.

"I guess it'd be about right," Bella said slowly. "A

hundred would be travel money, enough to get me to some-place where Dutch ain't likely to find me."

"All right, we have a deal," Jessie nodded. "Now that we've agreed on a price, when can we look at the letters?"

"Any time you're ready, I guess."

"Now's the best time," Monica put in. "We don't know when Dutch Ventner's likely to show up, Jessie. We want to be ready for him when he does, and we'll need to make some plans."

"Yes, of course," Jessie agreed. Turning to Bella, she asked, "You don't object, I hope?"

"Whenever suits you, suits me," Bella answered. "If you'd rather wait till later—"

"No," Jessie said. "We've spent a lot of time talking, and the afternoon's wearing on. There's no use wasting time. It'll be dark in another hour or so."

As Jessie dug into the pocket of her jeans she said to Monica, "Suppose I pay Bella what we've promised her and you and I square up later."

"If that's the way you'd like to handle it, it'll be fine. Go ahead."

Jessie took out the purse in which she carried her travel money and extracted five $20 gold pieces. As she handed the money to Bella, she told Monica, "I'll ask Ki to saddle my horse. He might even want to ride along with us."

"No!" Bella told her quickly. "Just you and me, Miz Starbuck. The fewest that knows about our deal, the less of a chance it'll be for Dutch to find out about it, too."

"Well, that makes sense," Jessie agreed. "All right. The two of us will go."

"You certainly must like privacy," Jessie said as Bella led the way out of the maze of huts and tents that made up the new town Dutch Ventner had started. "There are only three or four houses ahead of us."

"That's why I like the place I got," Bella replied. "Being rich the way you are, I don't guess you'd know what it's like, Miz Starbuck, working a dance hall night after night. A girl needs some peace and quiet."

"I'd never given it much thought," Jessie told her. "But I can see your point."

"Anyhow, that place over yonder's mine," Bella went on.

She pointed to a small shantylike cabin that stood well apart from the others at the edge of the new settlement. It was built of used lumber and had the look of having been thrown together by a left-handed carpenter working in the dark. They were approaching the cabin at its corner, and Jessie could not see the door. The "L" of a stovepipe stuck out its back wall and the only side wall that was visible was broken by a single small shuttered window. From its size, the shanty was large enough to contain only a bed, a small stove, and perhaps a chair or two.

"It ain't much," Bella added. "But all I use it for is to sleep in. If you been wondering, I do all my business at the Sunset. I don't bring it home with me."

Jessie could find no suitable response to Bella's explanation, and made none. They rode on, rounded the corner of the cabin, and Bella swung off her horse.

"Come on in," she said. "I got the letters in a box. It won't take but a minute to dig 'em out."

She was unlocking the cabin door as she spoke. Jessie dismounted and dropped the reins of her horse to the ground. She joined Bella, who was just opening the door. It swung inward, and Bella pushed it open wider.

"Go on in," she told Jessie. "I'll lock the door behind us, to make sure nobody walks in on us. Not that there's much chance that somebody'd come calling on me, but I got an idea you'd like to keep our deal sorta private."

"Of course I would," Jessie agreed.

Bella followed Jessie into the cabin. Jessie was looking around its interior, dim in the fading daylight that trickled through the grimy panes of the curtained window.

Jessie heard the hinges of the door squeak as Bella

101

closed it, and started to turn and add something to what she'd just said when a man's arm clasped her around the chest, holding her own arms motionless. At the same time, he closed the palm of his other hand over Jessie's mouth.

"Well, now," his sandpaper-rough voice grated in Jessie's ear. "It's about time we met up, Miss Starbuck. You been real busy asking folks about me. I figured I could tell you more'n you could learn second-handed, like."

Jessie had struggled only briefly when she felt the man's arm tighten around her chest. Behind her she heard the grating of the lock on the cabin door as Bella turned the key.

Jessie's first instinctive reaction had been to try to break free from her captor, but she'd had enough experience during the years of her battles with the cartel to know the value of conserving her strength instead of wasting it in a struggle that was doomed in advance to be futile. She forced herself to relax, but her mind was working at top speed.

Though she'd sensed the identity of her captor from the instant he'd grabbed her, Jessie got immediate confirmation when Bella spoke his name when the lock clicked in the door.

"Well, I got her here for you all right, Dutch," the dancehall girl said. "Now what're you going to do with her?"

"Don't worry," Ventner replied. "Just help me find some rags and a rope. I'll be easier to handle her after I get her gagged and tied up."

"Remember what you promised me," Bella said. "You're just gonna leave her here while me and you makes our getaway."

"Sure I remember," Ventner replied as he shoved Jessie down on the bed that filled most of the small one-room cabin.

Jessie got her first look at Dutch Ventner then, as she

managed to twist her body around after she'd landed on the bed.

He was a big man, though not a tall one. Even in the dim light that trickled into the cabin from its single dirt-streaked window, she could see his heavy eyebrows and the dark reptilian eyes below them. The scars of smallpox pitted his unshaven cheeks. Ventner's nose showed the twists of broken bone and cartilage that marked him as a fist-fighter as well as an outlaw and gunman. He wore a thick checked wool shirt and miner's jeans, with a wide gunbelt supporting a holstered revolver.

"Well, if we're going to get away, we better go, then," Bella said. "Nobody's going to think about looking in this cabin for a day or two, so we'll have a good start."

"I guess we would," Ventner agreed. "But I been thinking things over, Bella. I can use the Starbuck woman to make a lot of money. You ain't no use to me no more."

Before Bella had really grasped the meaning of his words, and before Jessie had divined what the outlaw intended, Ventner drew his revolver and shot Bella dead.

Chapter 10

"Jessie should've been back before now." Ki frowned as he looked out the kitchen window at the gathering dusk.

"Perhaps not, Ki," Monica replied. "There may have been a lot more than we expected in those letters Bella has."

Ki nodded. "That's possible. But Jessie's not one to waste time, and she's been gone long enough to read two or three dozen letters."

"I'm sure she has, but just because she hasn't shown up yet doesn't necessarily mean she's wasting time. She might've stopped for a minute to talk to Sid and Annie, to find out about something that she ran across when she was reading those letters Bella has."

"I hadn't thought of that," Ki replied. "But I suppose it's possible. Just the same, I think I'll saddle up and ride toward town. Jessie and I have gone through a lot of things together, and I don't usually worry about her unless my instinct tells me there may be something wrong."

"You surely don't think Jessie's in trouble?" Monica asked, a puzzled frown on her face now.

"Not necessarily. Just a precaution. You don't mind staying here alone for a little while, do you?"

"Goodness, no! Remember, this house used to be my home, Ki. It's where I grew up. I'll be all right."

"Of course you will." Ki nodded. "And probably Jessie is, too. But I'll go meet her, just the same."

Ki made short work of saddling his livery horse and starting toward town. The deep blue of night was tingeing the eastern sky by the time he was within sight of the Bennet's store, and Ki frowned when he did not see a light showing inside the building. He reached the hitchrail, tossed his horse's reins on the crossbar, and went inside.

Though the bell on the door had tinkled as Ki closed it, neither Sid nor Annie appeared through the back curtain. A worried frown creased Ki's brow as he walked to the curtain and pulled it aside. From the doorway where Ki had stopped, he could look into the bedroom.

Sid was lying in the big double bed. His head was swathed in a bandage that covered his chin and nose, and in the slit that had been left open for his eyes Ki could see that his eyelids were closed. Annie sat slumped in a rocking chair beside the bed. Her eyes were also shut, her hands folded in her lap. Ki looked at her more closely and saw that one of her hands protruded from the triangle of a sling. For a moment he thought both of them were dead; then Sid's face twitched in pain.

"Sid?" Ki exclaimed. "Are you all right?"

Sid's eyes opened. He turned his head as though each small move he made pained him. When he saw Annie in the chair beside the bed he called her name, his voice grating hoarsely.

"Annie seems to be asleep, Sid," Ki said quickly. "If you want something, I'll be glad to help you."

Unexpectedly, Annie spoke. "I'm awake now." Her

voice was weak and querulous. "I just closed my eyes for a minute."

"What's wrong?" Ki frowned.

"It ain't nothing, Ki," Sid replied. "I'm just so old I'm getting clumsy and I fell down and hurt myself."

"You surely don't expect me to believe that," Ki told him. "Not when I can see that big bandage on your head. You couldn't have hurt yourself badly enough to need that much binding up."

"It's the truth, Ki," Sid insisted. "I got my legs all twisted up in my cane and taken a bad tumble."

"And what about you, Annie?" Ki asked. "I suppose you fell down and hurt your arm while you were trying to help Sid?"

"That's just what happened, Ki," Annie replied. "I was in a hurry, and I got the clumsies."

Ki shook his head as he said, "You must think I can't tell the difference between what you've been telling me and what I'm sure must be the truth. Now, stop trying to fool me, and tell me why I found you both out here with the store door unlocked and no lamp lighted. Don't you realize that anybody could come in here and walk off with whatever they wanted and you'd never know a thing about it!"

"We ain't going to fool Ki, Annie," Sid told his wife. "And I guess we better tell him. If Jessie Starbuck thinks enough of him to trust him, we oughta be able to."

"You go on and tell him, then," Annie said. "I'll bust in if you leave out anything."

"Dutch Ventner's got back to town, Ki," Sid began. "And he's got wind of you and Jessie nosing around. He knows I used to work for Alex Starbuck, and he's found out me and Annie was talking to you and Jessie. He ain't sure what you're after, but he's got the idea that the two of you come here to make trouble for him."

"Which we did." Ki nodded. "How much did you tell him?"

"Me and Annie didn't say a word," Bennet replied. "We let on like you didn't tell us a thing about why you come here."

"That's when Dutch began beating on Sid and me," Annie put in. "But we still didn't tell him a thing about you and Jessie, or let on about that congressman asking you to come up here."

"Did Dutch know about that dance hall girl?" Ki asked. "Or that Jessie was at her place talking to her?"

Sid shook his head. The movement must have been painful, for his face contorted and he slumped back on the pillows. His voice weaker than before, he said, "If he did, he didn't let on. All he done was knock Annie and me around a little bit more, then he taken off."

"And Jessie didn't stop by here?" Ki asked.

Again Sid shook his head. "We ain't seen her, Ki. Why? Has something happened to her?"

"I don't know yet. She went with that dance hall girl, Bella, to look at some letters that Ventner wrote when he and Bella were living together and she was helping him, acting as a lookout when Ventner robbed a bank, jobs like that."

"I know about that, o'course," Sid said. His voice was a bit stronger now. "Bella stood lookout on two or three jobs I went on with Dutch when I was in cahoots with him."

"Do you know where Bella's cabin is?" Ki asked. "Jessie told me before she left the Ransom's place that she was going there with Bella."

Sid shook his head, but Annie answered, "I know she rented a cabin someplace away from the Sunset so's she could get away from there after she'd finished working. But she never did say where it is."

"I guess maybe the barkeep at the Sunset would know," Sid put in. "He'd be the only one outside of Dutch that might."

"Thanks, Sid." Ki said. "That's where I'll head for,

then. Now, is there anything I can do to help you and Annie before I leave?"

"We'll make do all right by ourselves, Ki," Annie said. "We ain't used to doing much leaning on other folks. But it's nice of you to offer. You go on and find Jessie."

"If she should stop by here on the way to the Ransom place, you might tell her I'm looking for her," Ki told the couple as he turned to go. "I'll stop at the Sunset and find out where Bella's cabin is. I'm pretty sure Jessie will still be there, but I'm not taking any chances."

In the instant before the loud clap of Ventner's gunshot broke the quiet air of the little cabin, Jessie moved. She was rolling off the bed to the floor as the impact of the heavy .45 slug from Ventner's gun sent the dance hall girl sprawling onto the bed where Jessie had been lying.

Jessie's hat scraped the bed as she dropped, and the brim was pushed down over her eyes. She reached up and pushed it away as she hit the floor and then reached for her Colt, but she'd fallen on her right side and the gun was under her hip. Her weight resting on the pistol's holster combined with her ungainly position defeated even her quick reflexes. Before she could roll onto her back and free the weapon, Ventner was standing over her, the muzzle of his revolver only inches from her face. She stayed motionless.

"Don't try it!" Ventner snarled. "I ain't wanting to kill you, but I sure as hell will if you put your hand on that gun!"

Jessie had learned very early that a sure path to suicide was to try to draw a holstered revolver while a skilled gunfighter had her covered. She let her gun hand drop to her side and remained motionless.

Ventner nodded. "That's better. But I'd feel a lot better if you didn't have that fancy pistol so damn handy."

Reaching down, he closed his left hand around the butt

of Jessie's Colt and snaked it out of its holster, thrusting the weapon into the belted top of his breeches. Then he stepped away from Jessie and stood looking at her, his gun rock-steady, its muzzle only a yard or two from her eyes. Ventner looked at her as though he was examining an alien form of life from some distant planet.

"You'd be the Starbuck woman," he went on. "I've heard old Sid Bennet yak-yakking about you till I'm sick of it. I guess you're pretty enough, but I've seen better."

"I'm sure you have," Jessie replied, her voice coolly casual. "And I've seen a lot better men than you."

"At least you got enough spunk to talk back." Ventner grinned. "I just bet I'm gonna have a lot of fun taming you."

"Don't bite off more than you can chew," Jessie warned him.

She kept her voice level.

"I ain't in the habit of doing that," Ventner replied.

Jessie noted the sudden change in his voice, and racked her brain to think of a way to distract Ventner long enough for her to escape. Cold logic told her that if the outlaw intended to kill her, he'd have shot her the instant after his slug had cut down Bella. In spite of her efforts, she could think of nothing that would draw his attention away from her. She'd been in tight spots before, but seldom one as tight as this, lying weaponless and vulnerable on the floor of the cabin with Ventner holding his pistol less than a yard from her head. In that moment she decided that she had only one course to follow, and that was to obey her captor's orders for the moment, until a chance to get away presented itself.

"Stand up now and stick your hands out in front of you," Ventner commanded suddenly. "And hold 'em together while I find a rope or something to tie you with."

"I get the idea that you intend to take me away with you," Jessie said as she got to her feet, playing for time, hoping to delay Ventner's move as long as possible. She'd been well aware of her danger since Ventner first made his appearance. Now, as the sole witness to his brutal murder of Bella, Jessie knew that her situation was even more precarious than before.

"You don't think I'd be a big enough damn fool to leave you here, do you?"

Ventner answered without looking at Jessie. His eyes were flicking around the sparsely furnished room, looking for rope or cord with which to tie her. He saw the curtained corner behind the door where he'd hidden, and backed toward it, keeping the muzzle of his revolver aimed at Jessie. Reaching through the curtains, his eyes still on Jessie, he pawed around in the little corner. A satisfied grin spread over his face as he brought out a corset.

"Now, this is just the ticket!" Ventner said. He tossed the corset on the bed beside Bella's body, ignoring the corpse, his eyes still riveted on Jessie, while he pawed the corset laces from the undergarment's eyelets. He worked by feel, still keeping his eyes on Jessie.

As he pulled the long laces out, Ventner went on, "I've pulled these damn strings tight too many times not to know how tough they are." Then, as he finally freed the laces, he stepped toward Jessie and commanded, "Now, hold your hands still while I get you bound up. I've heard too much about you from Sid to take any chances on letting you get loose."

Jessie had no alternative. She stood quietly while her captor wound one of the long laces around her wrists, looping turns now and then over her thumbs and fingers until Jessie's hand were held together so tightly that she could not flex her fingers after he'd tied the ends of the cord.

"That'll hold you for sure," Ventner said as he tied off the knot and stepped away from Jessie. He went to the single small window and pulled the curtain aside a cautious inch. Jessie looked past him, and saw that the sky was almost dark.

"Just don't make no trouble for me now, and we'll get along all right," Ventner told Jessie. "It's dark enough for us to ride outta town without nobody paying us any mind. Come on."

With Ventner pulling her along by her tightly bound wrists, Jessie had no choice. He held the stirrup of one of the horses and she slid her foot into it, then, since she could not grasp the saddle horn for leverage, he lifted Jessie by the waist and settled her into the saddle. Bending over, he began lashing her foot into the stirrup. When he'd finished the job to his satisfaction, the outlaw stepped back and inspected his work.

"That oughta hold you tight," he told Jessie. "You just keep in mind that you can't get that foot outta the stirrup. You try to slip off that horse and you'll get dragged. I guess you've seen what dragging does to a rider that's got his foot jammed."

"Yeah, I've seen it," Jessie replied, her voice studiedly casual. She recalled the times when one of the riders at the Circle Star had been bucked off his horse and his boot had jammed in one of the stirrups. Always the dragged man's face had been a pulped mass of bleeding skin when the other hands managed to free him.

"Then you ain't going to try no fancy tricks while we're on the trail," Ventner said over his shoulder as he swung into the saddle of the second horse. "Now let's ride. We got quite a ways to go to get where we're heading."

Riding toward the town's sprawled-out buildings under the deepening blue of the after-sunset sky, Ki pulled up at the barnlike building that bore the scrawling sign *Sunset Saloon & Dance Hall* above its wide batwings. Looping the reins of his livery horse around the hitch-rail, he pushed through the batwings.

At that early hour, the night had not yet begun for the saloon. Three or four early drinkers were elbowed up to the long bar that spanned one entire side of the cavernous interior, and at its far end a single barkeep stood polishing glasses with the big dishtowel that served him for an apron. No bar-girls were in the place, nor were any customers seated at the tables that surrounded the small, square dance floor in the center of the building.

Ki walked down one wall to the end of the bar where the barkeep was working.

"You might as well turn around and get the hell outta here," the barkeep said before Ki could speak. "We don't serve no Chinks. House rules."

Ki looked at the barkeep for a moment without replying. The man had a protruding jaw; the beginning of a double chin failed to hide its square blockiness. His high cheekbones were made even more prominent by layers of scar tissue which did not quite match the leaden hue of the skin around them. The heavy brows which gave his eyes a piglike look and caused his forehead to appear backslanted failed to hide the thin white weals that identified him as a professional pugilist.

"I am not Chinese," Ki said levelly. His level tone carried neither surprise nor anger. "I am of Japanese ancestry."

"That don't make no difference," the barkeep replied. "You got a snubby nose and slanted eyes, so as far as I'm concerned, you're a damn Chink. We don't serve your kind here, so go on and git out!"

"I have not asked you to serve me liquor," Ki went on, stifling his anger, as he'd learned to do long before now. Speaking in a low, level voice he said "I am looking for information."

"Damned if you ain't a little bit stupider than most of your kind," the barkeep frowned. "I told you two times that Chinks ain't allowed in here, and that's all I got to say! Now, git your yellow face the hell outside like I told you to, or I'll step out from behind the bar and throw you out on your butt!"

"It will do no harm for you to take a moment to answer

my question," Ki went on, still holding his rising anger in check and keeping his voice level. "I merely want to know—"

"Don't claim I didn't give you a chance to git!" the barkeep half shouted. "But you go on making like you're deaf, like you can't even hear me!"

Throwing down the glass he'd been polishing and paying no attention to the small, tinkling crash it made as it broke on the bar, the man let his apron fall and advanced on Ki, his forearms raised boxer-style, his hamlike hands closed into fists.

Ki did not move, though only a bit more than a yard separated him from the irrational, irritated barkeep who not only towered head-high over him, but who outweighed him by perhaps twenty pounds.

Growling with inarticulate anger, the barkeep launched a left-hand roundhouse punch, which Ki deflected with a quick *koken-ue* block. Snarling now, the barkeep threw a counterpunch with his right fist—a jab rather than a swinging blow. Ki met the onrushing fist with *shotei-ue* thrust of his right hand. The barkeep's knuckles slid off Ki's rock-hard palm while the force of his swing sent him forward, off balance.

Ki swivelled aside as the barkeep stumbled ahead, bending at the waist. Before the other man's momentum slackened, Ki grabbed his antagonist's head and pulled it downward as he brought up his leg in a *hiza-geri* kick that ended with the barkeep's head smashing into Ki's lifting knee. The man's thinly fleshed forehead met the bony knob of Ki's knee with a sharp crack, and he sagged to the floor, his eyes blinking, his arms and legs limp.

Ki's encounter with the barkeep had lasted less than ten seconds. The blear-eyed barflies at the opposite end of the mahogany either had not noticed the quickly ended fracas, or had ignored it, for none of them moved. Ki bent over the half-conscious barkeep, his mouth only inches from the man's ear.

114

"Before I am really angry, tell me where I can find the woman named Bella," he said, his voice icy cold.

"W-wu-west edge of town," the barkeep mumbled between grunts of pain. "A little shack off by itself. What paint's left on it's sorta blue. Now for God's sake get outta here and leave me be!"

"Thank you," Ki replied courteously. "If we meet another time, I hope it will not be necessary to persuade you so forcefully to reply to a simple question."

Releasing the barkeep's arm, Ki let it fall to the floor. He walked to the batwings and pushed and pushed through them without looking back, mounted his horse, and started for the western end of town.

A half arch of deepening blue still rose above the horizon ahead of him. Ki toed his horse into a faster walk, looking for the isolated cabin the barkeep had described. He was sure he'd found it when he made out the bluish hue of its walls. A frown grew on his face when he saw no horses outside, but he rode on steadily and dismounted in front of the little shanty.

Ki's frown deepened when he saw that the door stood ajar. He pushed through it and went inside. The dying day had not yet drained all the light from the cabin's interior. All Ki saw at first was Bella's body sprawled across the bed, a dark stain of dried blood clotting on her breast.

Chapter 11

For a moment Ki stood without moving, staring at Bella's corpse. Then he began looking around the room, seeking some sign that might give him a clue as to what had become of Jessie. In the light that was quickly fading to darkness, he examined the cabin inch by inch. The only object he found that seemed unusual or out of place was the laceless corset that lay on the floor beside the bed.

Ki picked it up and examined it, but aside from the fact that the laces had been removed, the corset gave him no message. At last he went outside and began searching the ground in front of the door. Daylight had gone almost completely now, and the scuffed, shadowed earth gave up no clues. In spite of the urgency that was driving him, Ki finally admitted to himself that he was wasting time. Mounting his horse, he rode back through the scattered shanties, heading for the Ransom house.

As he approached Sid Bennet's store Ki saw lights shining through the windows of the rooms in which Sid and

Annie lived. He reined in, dismounted, and tried the front door. It was locked. He knocked, and a few moments later Annie opened it.

"I was sure hoping you'd be bringing Jessie back with you," she said. "Was there any sign of her?"

Ki shook his head. "She was gone. It was too dark for me to make sense out of the hoofprints around the cabin, but I'm sure that Ventner found her and Bella there."

"Then Bella was still there?"

"Bella was dead, Annie. She'd been shot. I'm sure Ventner found her and Jessie together. After he killed Bella he must've taken Jessie somewhere with him. I'm hoping Sid can give me some idea where they might've gone."

"Well come on in, Ki," Annie invited. "Sid ain't in real good shape, but I know he'll try to help you."

"I'm sure he will, but is he strong enough to talk?"

"He could be a lot better. Just don't get him all stirred up, and don't stay too long. That roughing-up Ventner gave him took an awful lot out of him."

Annie stepped back from the door. Ki went in and followed her through the store to the back rooms. The bedroom door was standing open and Sid still lay in bed. He looked at Ki silently and asked the question with his eyes.

"Jessie's gone, Sid," Ki told the old man. "I'm afraid Ventner's got her. I couldn't make much out of the hoofprints in front of the cabin; it was too dark."

"Did Bella say it was—"

"Bella's dead," Ki broke in bluntly. "From what I could see at her cabin, Ventner must've shot her. Then I'm sure he took Jessie away with him."

Annie broke in. "Think hard, Sid," she urged. "You'd know a lot more than anybody else about where Dutch might be heading with Jessie."

Bennet did not speak for such a long time that Ki thought he might not have understood them. He began again. "What about Ventner, Sid? Do you have any idea at

118

all where he could have been heading?"

"I heard every word you said before, Ki," the old man replied. His voice was a rasping whisper and he spoke very slowly. "I ain't forgot what you asked me. But that beating I taken from them thugs has left me sorta addle-brained."

"Take all the time you need to think," Ki said. "It's already too dark for me to do anything tonight. But I'd like to start trying to find Jessie as soon as the sky's bright enough for me to see hoofprints, and it'll help if I've got some idea which direction I need to start looking."

This time, Sid replied almost at once. His voice was still faint, and his words came slowly as he said, "Seems like I do recall something Dutch said about having two hideouts. He was bragging to me one time right after me and Annie come here. We was talking about how it used to be when him and me as dodging the law."

A fit of wheezing interrupted Bennet's flow of words. He coughed and hawked, his body shaking. Then he sagged back on his pillow, his eyes closed. Ki waited patiently. After a few moments, the old man opened his eyes.

"It's come back to me now," he told Ki. "Dutch was sorta making a joke. We was talking about the hideouts we used years back, when me and him was riding the owlhoot trail. He said something like he didn't have to worry none about hiding from the law, said if they found his hidey-hole on the Kootenai, he'd let the gospel-shouters keep him safe. He didn't say no more, but I sorta got the idee he'd struck up a deal with a minister."

Ki frowned. "That doesn't make much sense. Dutch Ventner is the last man on earth I'd expect to go running to a preacher."

"That's what struck me," Sid replied. "And there sure ain't no churches hereabouts, nor no preachers I can think of closer than way to the south, down at Coeur d'Alene."

Ki shook his head and said, "It's not likely Ventner would head south, Sid. That's where towns and people are.

119

He'd be heading north, up into Canada, or west. I don't think he'd go east, unless he's got a hideout in the mountains."

"It's almost a hundred miles to the Bitterroots," Sid said. "Dutch'd have him a place closer to here."

"I'm sure he would, too," Ki agreed. He looked at Sid, who'd closed his eyes and was apparently dropping off to sleep again. Then he turned to Annie and went on, "I won't bother you and Sid any more now, Annie. He needs to rest, and I left Monica Ransom alone out at her house. She's probably wondering what's happened to me."

"I expect you'll be starting out to find Jessie when it's daylight?" Annie asked as she and Ki walked toward the front door. "I sure hate to think of what that rotten scoundrel might figure to do to her."

Ki nodded. "So do I. I'll find her, though, Annie. I'm not sure how much of a trail Ventner left, but I won't stop until I've followed it to the end!"

"And that's about all I know, Monica," Ki concluded his recounting of the blank wall he'd run into after finding Bella's body in her cabin. "I don't suppose the corset I found means anything, except that Bella had taken it off and didn't put it away."

"Did she have one on?" Monica asked.

"I don't know." Ki frowned. "When I saw she was dead, I didn't touch her or anything. I didn't even stop at the Sunset Saloon on my way back to tell whoever's in charge of the place that Bella was dead. I suppose I should have. Unless Dutch Ventner shows up again pretty soon, I imagine the man who runs the Sunset will have to take care of burying her."

"You're going back at daylight to try to pick up her trail, aren't you?"

"Of course I am! Two horses have surely left some kind of trail, and when I pick it up, I'll follow it until I find them!"

120

"We'll follow it together," Monica said. Her voice was low, almost subdued. Ki started to protest, but before he could speak she went on. "Save your objections, Ki. I won't listen to them."

"I wasn't really going to object," Ki frowned. "You just took me by surprise."

"I don't suppose I can take Jessie's place, because from what she's told me the two of you have faced some pretty ticklish situations together," Monica continued.

From the easy flow of her words, Ki judged that she'd been making up her mind while listening to him recount what he'd discovered in Bella's cabin.

"Nobody could ever take Jessie's place, Monica," he told her. "But I think of her as my family, just as I came to feel that Alex Starbuck was my father. And when Alex was murdered, she turned to me for help. Everything else has just followed naturally."

"I didn't ask Jessie this, because I haven't known her long enough," Monica went on, "but you're not lovers, are you?"

Ki shook his head. "No. There could never be a romance between me and Jessie. She's like a sister to me, one whom I treasure dearly, but not in the way you mean."

"I'm not sure I understand completely, but I'll keep trying. And as for me going with you to look for Jessie, there just isn't any way you can stop me. Besides, I know the country around here and you don't. And even in the short time I've known Jessie I've come to like her tremendously."

Ki's eyes had opened wide when Monica started speaking, but by the time she'd finished he realized that her knowledge of the country could be invaluable.

"After what you've said, I'm certainly not going to argue with you," Ki told Monica. "But you may be getting into something more dangerous than you imagine."

"I doubt it," she replied. "Even if I was just a little girl when Father and Mother settled here, it wasn't what you'd

121

call tamed country. We didn't have Indians to fight, but there were as many outlaw gangs around here, dodging the law in the States, as there are today."

"You don't have to explain, Monica," Ki said. "I'm not arguing. I just want to be sure you understand the danger."

"Suppose we say I do and let it go at that," Monica replied "Now, you said something about starting in the morning at daybreak. I'll be ready to go as soon as it's light enough to see."

With her wrists bound together and one foot tied in the stirrup of her horse, Jessie realized that she had no chance of breaking away from Ventner. She reconciled herself to the fact, and did the next best thing that occurred to her under the circumstances, memorizing any landmark which might help her find her way back to the settlement. Darkness soon forced her to give up that effort as the almost invisible trail over which her captor was leading them was swallowed up in the gloom.

Stars soon appeared in the night sky, but there was no moon and the jagged mountain-cut rim of the horizon was the only landmark that Jessie's eyes could find in the darkness. She studied the broken skyline for a short while, then suddenly realized that her efforts to memorize its features were useless. The strain of watching had tired her, and she began to sway in the saddle.

If Ventner was bothered by riding through the darkness, he gave no indication of it. Now and again Jessie saw the gleam of his face, ghostly white in the moonless night, as he glanced back at her, but for the most part he ignored her. He kept the horses moving at a steady pace, and from their slow, deliberate progress Jessie guessed that they had a long way to travel.

By now the shock of seeing Bella murdered and that of her own capture by Ventner was ebbing. Suddenly Jessie realized that she was very tired. She caught herself dozing in the saddle several times, and forced herself awake. She

122

was aware that time was passing, but she had no reference to go by that would tell her how long she'd been in the saddle. As still more time passed she grew tired of fighting nature and dozed more often, until a sudden change in the trail brought her awake. Her horse was no longer ambling along at a gentle pace. It had stiffened its legs, and she was jolting in the saddle now as the animal fought the sharp downslope of the trail.

Suddenly wide awake, Jessie straightened up and rode erect in the saddle. She became aware of a new sound, the murmur of rushing water, and realized as the noise grew louder that they had now entered a canyon which had a river at its bottom. The gentle burbling of the stream indicated that it was not a turbulent river, but one that flowed gently, down an easy slope. Through the close-growing trunks of the pine trees ahead she began to catch an occasional glimpse of the river, its surface gleaming black under the moonless night sky.

They'd covered only a mile or so when the gleam of sky on the river vanished, though Jessie could still hear the sound of rushing water. It faded and grew louder in turn as whatever path Ventner was following took them in a weaving course through and around stands of pines. Under the branches of the trees, the darkness was even more intense, and Jessie lost her bearings completely. Then a flicker of light stabbed through the night's gloom, and after they'd travelled a dozen or more yards forward the whisper of running water could be heard again.

Her ears attuned to the quietness that had been broken only by the soft rustling of the light breeze through the branches of the pines and the babbling of the stream, Jessie jumped when Ventner raised his voice in a sudden shout.

"Bracer!" he called. "Marty! Don't get spooked, now!"

"All right, Dutch!" a man's voice answered. "We been looking for you since dark, so you didn't surprise us none."

They'd travelled only a short distance further when Jessie saw a flicker of light ahead. A few minutes later the trees thinned and the reflections of the light ahead flickered off the surface of a small creek. There was a strip of clear space between its bank and the trees. Ventner turned the horses to follow the stream, and within another few minutes they reached a clearing that was bathed in the amber glow of light cast by a lantern that hung from a low branch of one of the trees.

At the back of the clearing Jessie saw the raw wooden walls of a small shanty. A ring of flat riverbed stones circled a firepit in front of the structure. Hunkered down at the edge of the firepit a man was breaking up dry twigs and tossing them on the darkening coals that smouldered in the pit. He leaned forward to fan the coals with his hat and the twigs sent up a few thin puffs of smoke before bursting into flames. Jessie blinked in the sudden light. Then her vision cleared and she quickly took stock of her new surroundings.

Ventner was swinging out of his saddle. The man starting the fire was tossing wrist-thick branches on the growing blaze. A second man, dressed as roughly as the first in covert-cloth jeans and a flannel shirt, was walking toward her and Ventner. Both he and the man beside the fire had short, untrimmed beards and both wore gunbelts supporting holstered revolvers.

"We been looking for you to get back since sundown," the man advancing toward them said to Ventner. He glanced at Jessie and frowned, then turned back to Ventner and went on, "And we figured you'd bring Bella back, like you said you was going to."

Ventner was walking toward the fire, stretching his legs as he moved to get out the saddle stiffness. He said, "Bella's dead, Marty. She turned on me, and I had to shoot her. But you and Bracer don't need to worry. I promised you a woman, and I brought you one. We'll have to break her in, but that won't take long with all three of us here.

And when we tame her down, she'll be every bit as good as Bella."

"It doesn't look like anybody's been here since I left last night." Ki frowned thoughtfully as he and Monica approached Bella's cabin. "Let's rein in right now, Monica. It was too dark yesterday to try to follow the hoofprints of their horses. It'll easier now for me to pick them up if there aren't any other prints right in front of the cabin."

Reining in, they dismounted and started walking toward the little shantylike cabin. Ki kept his eyes on the ground as they approached it. The ocher-hued soil was hard and crusted, but he could see the scrapes of horseshoes plainly. There were too many short scraped spots for him to distinguish one from another.

"It's going to be a hard job, isn't it?" Monica asked.

"This close to the cabin it is," Ki nodded. "But as soon as we've taken a quick look inside, I'll start working in a circle and see what I can figure out."

"I don't suppose you can tell one of those marks from another just like it," she said, bending forward as they walked to examine the ground more easily. "I know I sure can't."

"About all I can tell is which way a horse was headed," Ki replied. "And whether it was walking or trotting or galloping. Not much more than that, on this baked dirt."

"How can you tell even that much? Like which way the horse was going?" she frowned.

"It's not hard. Horses scrape the dirt when they walk, and their shoes will leave a mark like a wide vee, with its point in the direction the horse is moving."

They'd reached the cabin by now. Monica said, "I don't suppose anybody's been here since you left, Ki. But I guess you can tell after we've looked inside."

Ki opened the door and glanced inside, then turned back to Monica. He told her, "As far as I can see, nothing's been disturbed. Bella's body is lying across the bed, so we can be pretty sure nobody else came here after I left."

"We'd better go inside and get it over with, then," Monica suggested.

"I've been thinking," Ki replied. "I didn't take time yesterday to look through Bella's things. Maybe there's nothing in them that'll help us, but I don't want to overlook even a slim chance. You're sure you want to go inside?"

"Ki, if you think I'll turn squeamish when I see a dead body, it's because you don't know me very well yet. I grew up in this country when it was even wilder than it is now."

Ki nodded, then said, "You'd probably see quicker than I would if there's anything inside that would help us. I took a quick look around yesterday evening, to see if I could find the letters Monica was going to show Jessie, but it was getting too dark to see much. Would you—"

"Yes, of course," Monica interrupted him. "You'd be better than I would at finding the hoofprints that Ventner and Jessie's horses must have left."

With a nod, Ki turned away, leaving Monica to examine the cabin. He started at the hoof-scuffed ground stretching away from the door, walked a dozen paces away from the cabin, then turned to circle around it. Several sets of hoofprints were scraped into the hard earth in the direction of the settlement, but only a few led in other directions.

Ki widened his circle. The number of hoofprints leading to or from the cabin were fewer now, and could be spotted more quickly. Two sets led west, away from the cabin. The marks showed that one of the horses was following the other, and this gave Ki the clue he needed. He noted the direction that prints took, then turned and hurried back to the cabin.

Chapter 12

"I'm pretty sure I've found the hoofprints left by the horses Jessie and Ventner were riding," Ki said as he entered the cabin.

Monica was standing beside the bed. She'd folded the coverlet over Bella's face and the upper part of her body. She was holding the corset in her hand, looking at it with a puzzled frown.

When Ki spoke, she looked up and said, "Good. I've gone through everything I could find to poke into, Ki. Her clothes were all hanging behind that curtain in the corner. There were a couple of boxes and a portmanteau under the bed, but that's all. Bella really travelled light."

Ki glanced at the portmanteau and boxes that were on the floor beside the bed and asked, "I don't suppose you found those letters that Bella promised to show Jessie?"

Monica shook her head. "All that was in the portmanteau was some underclothes, pantelettes and slips, two pairs of shoes, and a couple of handbags."

"I'm sure you looked in the handbags and boxes?"

"Of course I did! There was a little .22 pistol and about a hundred dollars in gold and silver in one handbag, the other one was empty. One of the boxes was full of cosmetics, lip salve and rouge and powder and perfume. There was some fake jewelry in the other one, cheap, shoddy stuff. But no letters."

Frowning thoughtfully, Ki said, "My guess is that there never were any letters, Monica. Telling Jessie that she had some was just an excuse to get her here. I'm sure Ventner framed the whole thing with Bella."

"And he was waiting here for Jessie." Monica nodded. "Yes, that must've been what happened, and I think I've figured out why this corset was on the bed by Bella's body. Ventner needed something to tie Jessie's hands with, so he took out the corset-laces to use. If you've ever tried to break a corset-lace, you'll know it's almost impossible."

"I'm sure you'd know more about that than I do," Ki told her. "I've never tried to break one." Frowning thoughtfully, he went on, "There's still one unanswered question in my mind, Monica. Who is the preacher Ventner mentioned to Sid Bennet, the one he said was going to provide him with a hideout?"

"I'm afraid I don't understand what you're talking about," she told Ki. "As far as I know, there's not a church or a preacher within a hundred miles of here."

"When I was talking to Sid, he remembered something Ventner had told him about having two good hideouts in this part of the Territory. One was somewhere along the Kootenai River, and the other one was with a preacher."

"That's impossible," Monica said. "When we were living here, my mother was always complaining about not being able to go to church because there weren't any, or any preachers or—" She stopped suddenly, her forehead wrinkling thoughtfully, then went on, "Ki. Do you think Ventner was talking about a minister or could he have meant something else? A priest, maybe?"

128

"All I know is what Sid told me. When Ventner was bragging about his hideouts to Sid, he said that one was on the Kootenai River, and the other was with a preacher."

"There's the Priest River," Monica said, her voice showing her uncertainty. "Could he have meant that?"

"How far are we from the Priest River?"

"About a half-day's ride. It's not very far west of here."

"Is it a big river? Does it run in a canyon?"

"Not very big. And there aren't any rivers in this part of the country that don't run through canyons part of their length."

"And is the country it runs through pretty wild?"

"I've never been there, Ki, but my father used to hunt along the Priest when I was a little girl. I can remember him talking about how rough it was along the river, so I guess it runs through the wildest kind of country you'd ever want to see."

"That's it, then!" Ki exclaimed. "The tracks I found outside led to the west. And unless I'm very wrong, we'll find that second hideout Ventner mentioned to Sid somewhere along the Priest River."

"We're going to look for her, I hope," Monica said.

"Of course!" Ki answered. "Just as soon as we get some provisions."

"We'll have to go back to the store, then."

"I'm afraid so. I'm as anxious to get started as you are, but if the country we're going into is as wild as you say it is, we'd be fools to start without taking along enough food to last two or three days. It'll only delay us an hour or so, and I want to talk to Sid. If he knows anything about Ventner's hideout, it may save us more time than we'll lose."

"What about Bella's body?" Monica asked as she and Ki got into their saddles. "We can't just leave her lying there while we go looking for Jessie."

"I'll ask Annie to go to the Sunset Saloon after we've got a two- or three-hour start and tell whoever's in charge of the place about her. She worked there, so I suppose it's up to them to take care of burying her."

Turning their horses back toward the settlement, they rode toward the ragtag town with the rising sun in their faces, both of them lost in their own thoughts of what the day might bring.

When Jessie heard Ventner promising her to his men, she was more angry than alarmed and more determined than ever to find a way to escape. She set her jaw determinedly as she studied the three renegades. They'd left her without making a move toward helping her off her horse, and had moved to the far side of the rekindled fire where they were standing close together in low-voiced conversation. She could hear only an occasional meaningless word when one of them raised his voice for a moment.

By now, the biting constriction of the tightly-knotted corset-string had caused Jessie's hands to swell and grow stiff. Tired of waiting to get off the horse, irritated by the chafing of her wrists, she called, "Ventner! If you're planning to keep me here, you'd better do something about looking after me. I need to get off this horse and get my hands free. They're so swollen now that I can't even feel them!"

Ventner had looked up when Jessie called his name. Now he stared at her for a moment, then replied. "I'll get around to you soon as me and the boys got our business settled. It ain't going to hurt you none to set there a few minutes more."

Choking back the angry retort that she was tempted to make, Jessie relaxed as much as possible and began examining her surroundings. The little clearing was lighted now by the flames of the fire, and she could see a bit of the clearing beyond the far corner of the crude cabin made of slit pine slabs that stood at its edge.

A branch-thatched shelter loomed beyond the cabin, and under it she could make out the rumps of two or three

130

horses. The darkness of the forest shut out what lay beyond. Jessie concentrated on studying the details of the clearing that were visible in the firelight. Between the shanty and the firepit a trail of sorts had been beaten out of the clearing, and the barely audible sound of rushing water told Jessie that the river must be in that direction.

Night hid the rest of her surroundings from her, and there was nothing else to look at other than the three men who were still standing talking. As she studied them, Jessie saw nothing unusual about them. Except for the fact that Bracer and Marty wore beards and Ventner was clean-shaven, there was little to distinguish between them. On the streets of the raw Western towns Jessie had visited, she'd seen many men who'd looked so much like the trio that all of them might have belonged to the same family.

Ventner glanced at Jessie while she was examining him and his companions. He said something to them. Bracer turned and walked around the cabin and disappeared into the horse-shelter. Ventner started toward Jessie and Marty followed him. When they reached Ventner's horse, Marty took off the saddlebags and turned back to the shanty while Ventner came on toward Jessie.

As he got within easy speaking distance of her he said, "I'm a lot sleepier than I am hungry, so I aim to grab a little shuteye. Unless your belly's real empty, I guess you could stand to do the same thing."

Jessie suppressed the sigh of relief she felt like letting out and said, "Since you've kept me on this horse for the last six or eight hours, what I'd enjoy most is just having my hands untied and getting out of this saddle."

"Well, there's four bunks in the shanty, so you'll have a place to sleep," Ventner told her. Then he went on, "I'm too wore out to mess around with you right now and break you in for the boys, and I sure as hell don't aim to give them first crack at a filly that's pretty as you are. There'll be plenty of time later, after I get rested a little bit."

"Don't be in a hurry on my account," Jessie replied, her

131

voice icy. "I'm sure I've met worse scum than you, but I can't remember when."

Grinning wolfishly, Ventner said, "Now, I always enjoy running into a woman with a little spunk! Damned if I don't feel like starting in on you right this minute!" When Jessie stared past him without speaking, he went on, "But I'll enjoy it a lot more when I'm fresh." He was taking a clasp knife from his pocket as he spoke. He slid the point under the corset-string that bound her foot into the stirrup and cut it, then unwound the ends to free her foot.

Jessie did not wait for Ventner to help her, but slid out of the saddle quickly in spite of her bound wrists. She said nothing, but extended her swollen hands to the outlaw. When Ventner severed the bonds that had confined her wrists for the past several hours, she felt nothing, but as her blood began circulating through the veins of her hands she was forced to clamp her jaw tightly to avoid showing the jabbing pain, like the piercing of a hundred needles, that shot through her fingers.

Marty came out of the cabin, carrying a pair of leg-irons. They were the new-style shackles, connected by a chain instead of an iron rod, and with a separate padlock for each leg shackle. As he reached the fire he said to Ventner, "Don't go forgetting who these belong to now, Dutch. I aim to keep 'em because they'll remind me of—"

"Of that deputy you killed with your bare hands over in Astoria so you could take the key off of him," Ventner broke in. "I've heard you tell that yarn so many times I could do a pretty good job of telling it myself."

"Well, you don't have to get so mouthy about it," Marty said angrily. "I ain't heard that you've done anything lately that'll match it."

"Maybe that's because I've learned not to blow so loud that everybody looks at me," Ventner shot back. "Now give me them leg-irons and the key. She don't seem to be hungry, so I'll put her in the cabin and chain her to the bunk. That way I'll be sure you or Bracer won't get to her before I do."

"And what're we supposed to do?" Marty asked, frowning angrily. "You told us that soon as you got back we was going to plan out that next job you said we'd pull."

"There'll be time for that, too," Ventner replied. "Just keep your pecker in your pants and we'll set it up. And if you and Bracer got any sense, you'll crawl into you blankets and sleep till daylight, like I aim to do."

Turning away from Marty, Ventner took Jessie by the arm and led her to the shanty. She blinked in the darknesss, which was absolute in the cabin. Then Ventner scratched a match on the door frame and lighted a lantern that hung just inside the door. Blinking again as the yellow lantern light revealed the interior of the hut, Jessie took stock of her surroundings.

There were no windows in the shanty, and its floor was packed earth. Its only door was the one they'd just entered. As she glanced around it, Jessie saw at once that the interior of the jerry-built cabin was more than spartan—it was downright bare. Its furniture consisted of a table made by nailing two planks across the top of a large log; the top slanted down a bit on one side. Other log-sections, shorter than the table, served as chairs.

Narrow bunks had been built on each wall. All four were wide enough to accomodate only a single occupant. Above and beside the bunks, with their tossed and wrinkled blankets, nails had been driven into the wall slabs. On three sides of the room, clothing and saddlebags hung from the nails. Those around one of the bunks were bare. No blankets were spread on the bunk, but two burlap feed sacks stuffed with some kind of dried leaves or vegetation lay on it end-to-end to serve as a mattress.

"I see you don't think much of our shanty," Ventner said as he watched Jessie's face while she examined her surroundings. "I got to admit it ain't all it oughtta be for a lady, but we don't run much to lady callers. The main thing is, none of what few lawmen we got around here's run onto it yet, and we don't use it only in the summertime. Nobody can get close to it in winter, so it suits us pretty good, for what it is."

When Jessie made no response to his long speech, Ventner's face twisted into an angry scowl.

"I seen a few like you before," he rasped, the corners of his wide mouth downturned. "Think you're too good for anybody but some la-di-da lily-fingered swell that puts on a clean shirt every week and struts around like he owned the world and all its people!"

Jessie stood wordless when the outlaw paused, and her continued silence angered him still more.

"Well, between me and Marty and Bracer we'll have you pulled right down to the ground before we're finished with you," he grated. "And maybe under it afterwards, for all I can tell. Now, lay down on that bunk where there ain't no clothes hanging and I'll put these leg-irons on you."

Still without speaking, she stepped over to the vacant bunk with Ventner following her. Preparing to lie down, Jessie turned just in time to ward off his hands with jabs of her elbows as he raised them to push her down onto the gunnysacks.

"I'll remember that when I start breaking you in," Ventner threatened. "You ain't the first one I've tamed! You just think about what you got coming while you're waiting!"

Jessie remained stubbornly silent as she sat down. Then she stretched out on the burlap sacks. Ventner's angry frustration seemed to have been relieved by his outbursts, for he said nothing more as he unlocked the padlocks of the leg-irons. He passed one of the shackles under the corner of the bunk so that the chain ran behind one leg, then closed the metal circlets around Jessie's booted ankles and snapped the padlocks into the hasps.

For a moment the outlaw stood beside the bunk looking

down at Jessie. Then he turned away and stepped to the door. As he opened it wider to look outside, Jessie got a glimpse of the other two outlaws, hunkered down beside the fire.

"I ain't telling you what to do," Ventner called to them. "But I sure won't be polite to anybody that wakes me up when they come in to doss down. You two just keep that in mind when you get ready to call it a day."

Slamming the door, Ventner blew out the lantern, and in the sudden darkness Jessie could hear the scuffing of his boots on the earthen floor as he crossed the cabin to his bunk. Ventner grunted and snorted two or three times. Then she heard the soft rustle of bedclothing. He began snoring almost at once.

Lying quietly, Jessie stared up into the darkness, her mind occupied with finding a way to escape the experience the outlaw had threatened her with when morning came. She had not moved and did not stir when the cabin door scraped open. By the trickle of light that filtered in from the coals of the dying fire she saw the silhouetted figures of both Marty and Bracer framed in the open doorway. When one of them spoke in a whisper, Jessie could hear him plainly in the night's stillness.

"Just don't make no noise," the outlaw said. "Even if Dutch is snoring loud enough to wake up a corpse, he always sleeps light. He's real mean when he gets roused up sudden, and you seen him chain up the woman with them leg-irons he made me give him. They'd clatter for sure if we try to get at her."

By his reference to the leg-irons, Jessie could identify the speaker as Marty. She lay quietly, motionless.

"Well, I'm sure as hell horny, but not bad enough to take a change of getting crossways with Dutch," Bracer whispered in reply to his companion. "We better just go to bed quiet and wait till tomorrow."

"Sure," Marty agreed. "And there'll be plenty of time then. Go on over to your bunk before I close the door. This

135

damn night air always gives me the wheezes."

Jessie saw Bracer's silhouetted figure and heard the faint whisper of his footsteps crossing the packed dirt of the floor. Even that small noise must have disturbed Ventner, for his snores became snorts for a moment, then with a final piglike grunt he subsided. In the silence the brushings of bedding sounded very loud indeed as Bracer settled in and pulled up his blankets.

Then Marty closed the cabin door and total blackness took over the interior of the shanty again. Jessie heard more soft whispers of fabric brushing fabric as Marty settled into his own bunk. After a few minutes of dead silence the night's quiet was again disturbed as one of the outlaws started snoring. Jessie could not identify the noisy one, or pinpoint the direction of the bunk from which the sounds came, but as they went on and on she decided that she had nothing to lose by making a bit of noise herself.

Flexing her hands to assure herself that they were no longer too stiff to move, Jessie sat up and then bent forward. She ran her hand from the top of one of her boots until her fingers touched the cold iron shackle that encircled her ankle. A bit of silent prodding told her what she'd hoped to find. Made to fit the ankle of a man, there was a finger's thickness of play between the shackle and her boot.

Encouraged, Jessie flexed her ankle, bending her foot forward until it was almost straight. Then she began twisting her foot and ankle from side to side, pushing down on the iron circle while she pulled her foot up. The squeeze was tight, but bit by bit, a half-inch at each twist, her foot slid up inside the boot, leaving the boot caught in the shackle.

Once her foot and leg were free, it was the work of only a few seconds to slip the boot's soft, flexible top out of the shackle. Greatly encouraged, Jessie set to work freeing her other foot in the same manner. Lowering the leg-irons silently to the dirt floor, she wasted no time. She thought of trying to retrieve her Colt, but even with Ventner snoring as he was, she judged the risk to be too great.

Tiptoeing to the door, Jessie carefully eased it open. Then she stepped outside, closed the door silently, and ran across the clearing into the dark pine forest.

Chapter 13

"What do you think, Ki?" Monica asked as Ki walked slowly back toward the spot where she'd been waiting with the horses.

"I don't just think that we've lost their trail now," Ki replied. "I'm sure of it. Somewhere behind us Ventner and Jessie turned off. It must've been on that last stretch of rocky ground that was too hard to hold tracks."

Until they'd crossed the two-mile-wide barren area where the hoofprints left by the horses carrying Jessie and Ventner had vanished, the trail had been easy for a tracker of Ki's skill and experience to follow. Over most of the area they'd covered, the tracks had led them through wooded country; great stands of centuries-old white pines that shaded the ground and inhibited the development of undergrowth.

During the uncounted years in which the tall trees had grown to maturity, the pines had also shed their needles generously. The pine needles covered the soil with layer after layer of slowly decomposing vegetation, a thick blanket of duff which, while resilient, had a fragile surface which the hooves of horses broke through and disturbed in their passing.

Although there were occasional places where the trail left by other horseback travellers who'd passed that way crossed the hoofprints of their quarry, it had been easy for Ki to distinguish the older prints from the newest ones, and pick out the hoofmarks he and Monica were following. Then, where the sun baked stretch of ground began, there were suddenly no hoofprints at all. Ki had chosen the best compromise he could think of, and had gone on in the same direction they'd been moving.

"Do you think you can find the place where Ventner and Jessie changed their direction?" Monica asked now, as Ki walked back to where she'd been waiting with their horses while he scouted on foot.

"It shouldn't be too much trouble," Ki said, swinging into his saddle. "I'll just have to do a little circling around. But backtracking is going to take time, and Ventner captured Jessie more than twelve hours ago. That's a lot of time for us to make up, Monica."

"About all we can do is track them, though," Monica said, her troubled frown matching the worried tone of Ki's voice.

"I wonder if it is," Ki went on, his voice thoughtful now. "From what Sid said, we're sure that Ventner's hide-out is somewhere along the Priest River, and we still haven't gotten to it. If we just go on until we reach the river, we ought to be able to follow it until we find Ventner's hidey-hole. It's sure to be close to the river-bank."

"You know more about things like this than I do, Ki. We'll do whatever you think is best."

Ki had been busy subtracting and adding hours and minutes in his head. Now he said, "I'm sure we'll save time by going on to the river. That's the best clue we've

140

got. Once we reach it, we'll turn upstream and ride along the bank. Even if we'll be riding a blind trail, it'll be faster than back tracking."

Monica nodded "Let's go ahead and follow the river, then," After a moment's thought. "Should we go upstream or down?"

Ki had already asked himself that question, and he replied to Monica without hesitating. "Upriver," he said. "From what you've told me, the country's less settled upstream, so Ventner would've picked that area to the north when he was looking for a place to set up his bolthole."

Without any further discussion, Ki and Monica started their horses moving and set out in the direction of the river.

When Jessie escaped from the cabin and started across the clearing, the rising moon had not yet gotten high enough to cast its light over anything but the tips of the tall pines. She moved quickly across the cleared area where the dying coals in the firepit shed a ghostly glow that plunged into the dark forest. After only a few steps across level ground she lurched forward precipitately as the ground dipped into a sudden steep slope and the soft tinkling of running water warned her to stop.

Though she was still too close to the shanty for her liking, Jessie halted and looked around until she'd located the stream she'd heard. It was only three or four steps ahead, a shining strip of water a dozen feet wide, blackened by night, but with bright points of starlight shining from its surface and defining its course. The creek was directly across her path, and in spite of her urgency to get as far from the shanty as fast as possible, she stood still while she debated whether to try crossing the stream in the darkness or following along its bank until it joined the river.

It was the water's inky blackness that made her choose to follow the creek-bank downstream, for nowhere on its surface could she see the froth of white water breaking over stones that would mark a shallow spot which she could wade safely. Jessie had spent enough time in the forested mountains where Starbuck lumbering camps were located to have learned that small, fast-flowing streams of the kind she was now looking at often had deep holes where some quirk of their current had scoured out the bottom to a depth of ten feet or more.

Turning to follow the creek's bank, Jessie started moving again. She'd heard no noise from the shanty, no voices raised in anger that would have warned her that the three outlaws had discovered her escape. She moved slowly and cautiously along the slanting ground that dipped to the water's edge. She wished that she dared to move faster, but knew that she could not risk hurrying over the strange terrain in the darkness. A single slip of her foot, a fall, or any other noise alien to the quiet forest would almost certainly wake up Ventner and his gunmen.

Along the banks of the little mountain stream the virgin firest grew down to the water's edge, but Jessie's night vision was good. As she weaved in and out around the boles of the high-towering pines, the only noise she made was the faint whisper of her footfalls on the soft forest duff.

Accustomed as she was to riding instead of walking, her legs began to ache as she plunged deeper into the thick forest. A windfelled tree lying across the creek bank stopped her after she'd taken fifty of sixty paces more, and Jessie sat down on it. After she'd been sitting motionless for a moment and the needles that were shooting through her legs did not go away she braced her hands behind her on the rough bark to balance herself while she raised her legs and stretched them out to ease her cramping muscles.

She heard a faint rustling noise behind her and started to turn, but before she could move a strong hand had grasped her wrists and pulled them together against her back, then held them in an iron grip. At the same time a hand darted out from behind and clamped her lips closed. Jessie started struggling to free herself, but no matter how hard she pulled against the hands of her unknown captor she could neither get her feet on the ground or braced on the bole of the fallen tree in a position that would allow her to use the full strength of her leg muscles to pull away from the vise-like grip of the unseen man.

"Just hold still," he said after a moment. The man spoke in a whisper, his lips close to her ear. "I know who you are, and I'm not going to hurt you. I'm sorry I had to grab you this way, but I didn't dare risk having you yell or say anything. Sounds travels a long way in this quiet night air, and we're still close enough to that outlaw hideout for them to hear you."

Jessie tried to nod, to indicate that she'd understood the stranger's words and motives, but his hand over her mouth kept her from moving her head.

"Now I'm going to let go of you," the man went on. "Just don't try to speak or ask any questions until we get far enough away from the outlaw camp to talk without rousing them."

Jessie nodded as best she could with the stranger's hand holding her head firmly. He felt the pressure of her effort and removed his hand from her mouth. At the same time, he released his grip on her wrists. Then his hand closed around Jessie's upper arm, and he helped her over the trunk of the fallen tree. Keeping his hold on her arm, he led her along the creekbed, away from the hideout where the outlaws were sleeping.

They'd travelled for perhaps a quarter of an hour before the stranger released Jessie's arm and stopped. She'd been able to get only fleeting glimpses of his face as they moved hastily through the obscurity of the deeply shadowed night, and now she turned to peer through the dappled moonlight and look at the man closely for the first time.

He towered a head above her, and enough moonlight trickled through the deep darkness of the virgin pine forest to enable Jessie to see that he was tall and sturdy and still young, quite likely in his early thirties, that he had a large, aquiline nose, and that his square jaws were darkened with the short stubble of a week-old beard.

"You don't have a thing to worry about now, Miss Starbuck," he said. Keeping his voice low, he went on, "My name's Blake Laird. I'm a sergeant in the Northwest Mounted Police. I've been after Dutch Ventner and his gang for almost six months now."

"All by yourself?" Jessie asked. "Against Ventner and two other men?"

"You're from Texas, Miss Starbuck," Laird said. "So I'm sure you've heard about the Texas Ranger who was sent to put down a rioting gang down there. When someone asked why they hadn't sent more than one man, the Ranger answered, 'Well, there's only one riot, isn't there?' Those of us in the Mounties have the same attitude."

"I've heard the story," Jessie told him. "And it could very well be true. Of course I'm familiar with the Mounties, but are we in Canada now?"

"We must be, or I wouldn't be here." Laird smiled. His face grew sober as he went on, "To be truthful, I don't know. The international boundary's marked by stone cairns a hundred miles apart and nobody knows where it goes, when the nearest marker might be fifty or more miles away."

"There's an agreement between Canada and the U.S., then?"

"Unwritten, but effective. When we're after a man we want badly, or your authorities are, we don't worry about borders. We just take our man to the nearest court, and your officials do the same thing. It saves a lot of legalistic folderol."

"I can see that it would," Jessie said, and nodded. "But I haven't even thanked you for helping me yet, and I do appreciate it. I'm also very curious about what you said a minute or two ago. How did you know about me?"

"I didn't know anything at all," Laird replied, "except

144

what I overheard while I was watching Ventner's camp, what he said when he brought you to his hideout. But I know the Starbuck name quite well from the interests in lumbering and mining your family has here in the Northwest provinces. This is where I've been stationed for the past seven years."

Jessie nodded. "Yes. My father was quite active in Canada as well as below the border."

"Your name didn't make any difference, of course," Laird said hastily. "I'd have helped you if you'd been named Susie Smith or anything else."

"You've been watching Ventner's hideout, then?"

"For more than a week now. I've been waiting to arrest them until Ventner joined them, so I could arrest all of them at the same time. I was watching them when Ventner brought you in, but I didn't arrest them then because I was afraid there'd be shooting, and you might've gotten hurt."

"So you came back to catch them asleep." Jessie nodded.

"Exactly," Laird replied. "Then I heard you moving around in the forest and thought it was Ventner or one of his men. When I realized it was you, I decided that I'd better get you safely away and go back to arrest the outlaws."

"In spite of what you said about the Mounties' attitude a few minutes ago, it'll be easier to take Ventner and his men if you have some help," Jessie told the Mountie.

"Are you suggesting that you want to help me?" he asked.

"I certainly am!" Jessie exclaimed. "I saw Ventner murder a woman in cold blood yesterday. I didn't know her well, but he simply killed her to get her out of his way, since she could've interfered with some of his plans. And the two men who're with him back there are just as bad, I'm sure."

"You'll excuse me, Miss Starbuck, but I'm not quite sure I know how you'd be able to help," Laird said.

"Situations like this aren't exactly new to me, Mr. Laird," Jessie told the Mountie. "And I'm a reasonably good shot—" She stopped short, remembering that Ventner still had her Colt and that when she'd ridden away from the Ransom house to visit Bella she had left her rifle behind. Shaking her head, she went on, "But I don't have a weapon of any sort now."

"It would be too dangerous anyhow," Laird said.

"I'm not a stranger to danger," Jessie said quickly. "And I can handle both a rifle and a pistol quite well."

"I'm sure you can, Miss Starbuck, but arresting Ventner and his men and taking them to prison is my responsibility. I can handle them without help."

"Even if I offer it?"

"Yes, of course. But I'll make us a cup of tea and dig into my jollybag for some food. Then we'll talk about what to do tomorrow before we get some sleep. It's only an hour or two until daybreak, you know.

"And there's no need for us to hurry, except to make sure that I get back to Ventner's hideout before he and his men wake up."

"They're going to wake up soon and find I'm gone," Jessie observed. "Then they'll spend the day looking for me. They'll probably split up, and then you'd lose your chance to capture all three at once."

"That hadn't occurred to me," Laird said. His voice was suddenly sober. "But you're right. By the time I take you to my camp and get back to the outlaw's cabin, they'll be scattered out, prowling through the forest."

"I can go ahead alone," Jessie said a bit hesitantly. "But I'd rather turn back and go with you now."

"No!" the Mountie replied firmly. "I'm responsible for your safety now, Miss Starbuck. I'll not risk your life by taking you with me when there's the risk of gunfight."

"What will we do, then?" Jessie asked. "Go on to your camp and spend the day, and attack the outlaws after dark?"

146

"You're a very persistent person, Miss Starbuck," Laird said. "You're still trying to get me to agree to take you back there with me, even though we're certain that there's going to be a gunfight."

"Of course I'm persistent!" Jessie agreed. "I'm not a china doll that has to be kept on a shelf! And I've been in gunfights before. My father was murdered by a group of men who were trying to seize financial control of the United States. When I inherited his holdings, they began attacking me. Ki and I finally defeated them, but it took a number of years and a lot of fighting."

For a moment the Mountie was silent. Then he said slowly, "I suppose I didn't realize that. Most of your fights were in the States, I suppose?"

"They were." Jessie nodded.

"And who is this Ki you mentioned?"

"Ki was my father's—well, I suppose the best description is the one I've used before, my father's right hand. He's now mine, and knowing him as I do, he's looking for me right now."

"In this wild country?"

"That won't matter to Ki. He's looked for me and found me in much wilder places than this."

"Perhaps I've been over-hasty," Laird admitted, speaking slowly and thoughtfully. "I wouldn't get back there until after sunup, and what you said a few moments ago is quite correct. By then Ventner and his men would be scattered out, looking for you. Night is the best time to take them, of course."

"Then you're ready to let me help you?"

"I'm not really sure that I should, but under the circumstances, I'll think about it."

"And what do we do now?" Jessie asked. "Go on to your camp and rest, so we'll be fresh tonight?"

"Yes. It's the best thing to do. And just in case I do change my mind about accepting your offer to help, we'd have to go there anyway, to get my rifle. Or, if you prefer,

147

I have a spare pistol that I bring on my field assignments."

Laird's words told Jessie that if he hadn't already made up his mind, he was very close to accepting her suggestion. She chose her words very carefully when she spoke.

"I'll be very glad to get some rest, Constable Laird, if you do agree to let me join you. But we can talk more about that later, after we get to your camp. Now, I've rested quite long enough. Shall we go on?"

"Maybe I should have done a more thorough job of scouting after we lost the trail," Ki told Monica as they reined in to let their horses breathe. "But I didn't realize how far we were from the Priest River, then."

"Neither did I," Monica replied. "And I suppose it's more my fault than yours that we haven't found it yet—the river, I mean. But it's a very winding stream, Ki. Like all the rivers up here, it flows south, but it has a lot of big bends, and it winds around to the west a lot."

"We've still got enough daylight left to cover quite a lot of ground," Ki said, glancing at the dropping sun. "But I hope we pick up their tracks before it gets too dark to see them."

He toed his horse ahead, and Monica followed his example. They moved on over the thickly forested terrain, Ki keeping his eyes open for any indications that they were close to the river. They'd been riding for a half-hour or more when the ground suddenly dropped away ahead. Ki pulled back on his reins and his horse slowed its pace. They reached the dropoff and looked down. Through the tops of the tall pines that grew thick on the floor of a wide valley below them, they saw the river at last.

"It's no wonder we haven't come across it before now," Ki said. "Look, it's flowing almost due west, and has been for almost as far as I can see."

"Eight or ten miles," Monica agreed.

"That explains why we haven't been able to pick up the trail Jessie and Venter must've left," Ki went on thoughtfully. "But it's not as bad as it seemed at first, Monica." He pointed to the wide-curving stream where it first came in sight at the head of the broad valley. "It's all downhill to the north. All we have to do is change our direction now, and ride in a straight line. We'll reach the river just about where it starts to curve. And if we're lucky, we'll cross the trail we're looking for before dark."

Encouraged by the sight of the river that had eluded them for so many miles, they toed their horses ahead and started down the long slope toward the sinuous line of the blue water.

★

Chapter 14

"I can understand now why Ventner turned north across that big bare spot where we lost his trail," Ki told Monica as he glanced at the sun, red now as it dropped closer to the rim of the canyon through which the river flowed. "His hideout must be quite a ways upstream, above this big bend we've been having to follow."

Monica nodded as she gazed up the wide winding canyon they'd been riding through since sighting the stream. "Yes. We've had to cover a lot of extra miles. But if we're lucky, we'll find where he's holed up before it gets too dark."

They'd spent more than an hour reaching the river after they'd sighted it again when they reached the end of the wide expanse of baked ground on which they'd lost Ventner's trail. Then they'd spent another hour or more riding north along the sweeping curve of its bank.

"It'd help if we had a landmark of some kind to look for," Monica went on as they passed a stretch of frothy white water and the noise of the current lessened.

"Sid didn't know any more than we did when he repeated that remark Ventner had made to him," Ki reminded her. "That was the only clue we had to go on. And we wouldn't have recognized it as a clue if you hadn't figured out what it meant."

"I certainly hope my hunch was right," Monica told him. "But my husband used to say my hunches were always pretty good."

Ki put aside the question he'd intended to ask Monica and comented, "I didn't know you're married."

"I'm not. Albert—my husband—died three years ago of typhus. That's one reason I came back here to look at our old family home. I had an idea that I might like to move into it."

"You say 'had.' Have you changed your mind?"

"I don't know, Ki. I certainly wouldn't want to live in it unless Ventner's crook hideout is torn down."

"I have a feeling that town of his won't last very long, Monica," Ki told her. "Because when he's caught, Jessie's eyewitness testimony that she saw him murder Bella is going to send him to the gallows."

"It's a wonder he didn't shoot her as well as Bella, to keep her from testifying against him if he got caught."

"I'm afraid he had a reason for taking her with him," Ki said. "And from what Sid's told me about Ventner, that worries me," Ki confessed.

While they'd talked, the ground along the bank had grown rockier. Ki glanced ahead and saw that they were drawing near another stretch of broken water. From the foaming, frothy surface of the river a wide expanse of stony, piled-up ground stretched in front of them. Ki looked at the forbidding surface ahead. The riffle was a wide one, and from the water's edge he could see that the expanse of piled-up stones and small boulders stretched to the wall of the canyon, three quarters of a mile away.

They'd had to cross such areas before, places where

over the years the riverbed had shifted, leaving broad expanses of loose boulders that had strewn the old streambed. In crossing such spots the hooves of their horses had slipped on the loose rocks, some as big as a man's head, which covered the ground from the edge of the river to the steep canyon walls. Hemmed in by the walls, they'd had little choice but to ride near the water's edge where the going was easiest.

They'd talked very little because for much of the way the sound of the stream's rushing water drowned out normal tones of speech and forced them to shout. In many places where the riverbed dipped precipitately and created rapids the noisy growl of the fast-rushing current was loud enough even to drown out the hoofbeats of their mounts.

Ki looked vainly for a trail that would lead them around or away from the expanse of loose stones, but saw none. He turned to Monica.

"I don't suppose we have much choice," he said. "This is another of those places we'll just have to let the horses pick their way across."

They reined their mounts to a slow walk as the animals began to shy when their hooves came down on the shifting stones. Both Ki and Monica were experienced enough to give the animals free rein to pick their own way over the treacherous stones. They'd almost reached the end of the uncertain footing when Ki's horse stumbled and almost went down. Ki dropped off the animal at once. The horse was whinnying shrilly, tossing its head and holding up its near front leg.

Ki stepped up to the animal's head, grasped the bridle's cheek-piece, and held it firmly. When the horse had calmed down, he bent to look at the hoof of the leg it was holding up. He pushed the leg down, but when it touched the ground the animal whinnied again and lifted its hoof in spite of Ki's downward pressure.

"It's either a sprain or a stone-bruise," Ki said over his shoulder to Monica. "I'll lead it past this bad stretch and maybe we can see exactly what's wrong."

Coaxing the horse with soothing noises, Ki managed to lead the animal over the remaining stretch of stone-covered ground. The horse moved hesitantly, dropping its near front leg now and then, trying to put weight on it, but pulling the leg up each time it made the effort.

Monica had led her horse across the stony stretch without difficulty, and had stopped on the clear ground beyond it. When Ki reached her he dropped to his knees and lifted his horse's hoof. Below the fetlock-joint the pastern was beginning to swell. Ki wrapped his hand around the swelling and squeezed lightly. The horse neighed and reared, pulling its hoof from Ki's hand. Then it dropped the hoof to the ground and started forward, only to lift its leg as soon as the injured joint felt its body's weight.

"It's not serious," Ki told Monica as he stood up. "Just a strain or sprain, but it's already starting to swell up. Right now the only thing I'm certain of is that I won't be doing any more riding today."

"I suppose we'll just have to stop, then," she said. "But do you think your horse will be able to carry you tomorrow?"

"I'm pretty sure it will," he said, looking up the valley in front of them. "There's brush growing just a little way from where these loose stones end. That's the nearest place I can see for us to stop for the night."

"We'd better stop there, then," Monica replied, looking in the direction Ki indicated. "Yes, and even from here I can see how green the ground is."

"Ride on ahead, then," Ki suggested. "It'll take me a little while to get there, leading this crippled horse."

"There's no need for you to walk," she said. "Ride on my horse's rump. I'll go slow enough for you to lead yours."

Ki led his limping horse to Monica's and vaulted onto its rump. Grasping the cantle of her saddle to give him leverage, he tugged at the reins of his horse. Reluctantly, the animal took a few halting steps forward. Monica toed her horse into motion. After they'd covered a few yards she turned her head to see how Ki was doing.

"You'd be in trouble if your horse balked, Ki," she told him when she saw his precarious grip on her saddle-cantle. "He'd pull you off. You need something more than my cantle to hold on to. Put your arm around my waist."

Ki realized at once that Monica's suggestion made good sense, for they still had a quarter of a mile to travel over the stone-studded ground. He released the saddle cantle and embraced her waist. He had to lean forward a bit to hold on, and his new position placed his lips only an inch or so from her ear.

"I'd better tether my horse near the river tonight and get up a few times to hold its foot in the water and rub it," he said. "That'll help reduce the swelling faster, and he ought to be able to carry me tomorrow without any trouble."

Monica turned to answer him, her cheek brushing across his lips as she moved. Ki pulled his head back quickly, but she paid no attention to their brief contact. She said, "A good idea, Ki. But if it's still lame in the morning, we can ride this way. It'd be a shame to have to stop, now that we must be getting close to Ventner's hideout."

"We must find that place tomorrow," Ki told her soberly. "The longer it takes us to find Jessie, the greater the danger she's in."

"I know." Monica nodded. "But even if your horse wasn't lame, we couldn't risk pushing ahead in the dark. We might pass the hideout and never see it."

Ki nodded his agreement, and she turned back to keep her eyes on the terrain ahead. After a quarter-hour of snail-slow riding they reached the grass-over spot, and Ki slid off the rump of Monica's mount. His own horse was limping badly now, and Ki wasted no time in unsaddling the animal and leading it into the cool, shallow water at the river's edge.

Hunkering down, he began rubbing and kneading and

squeezing the animal's swollen pastern-joint. The horse whinnied in protest at first and moved restlessly, but after a few minutes of Ki's patient attention it grew quiet and accepted the movements of his hands over the painful area. After he'd spent a quarter of an hour in the shallows, Ki tethered the horse to a big stone that protruded from the riverbed, stood up, and waded back to shore.

"I'm not sure I helped the horse's leg any," he told Monica as he reached the low-growing brush where she'd teethered her own mount. "But from the way it acted, its pastern didn't hurt as much as it seemed to when I started."

"All that we can do is wait and see how it is in the morning," she replied. Then, with a quick glance at the sun, which was already taking on its orangey before-sunset hue, she waved toward the bedrolls that she'd spread side by side on the ground nearby and went on, "It'll be dark by the time we eat a bit of supper. I thought I might as well get us ready for the night."

"A good idea," Ki agreed. "The ground around here doesn't look any softer than anywhere else, but at least it's got a little grass on it. And I'm certainly ready to eat supper. By the time we finish, my trouser legs will be dry, and I'll be ready to go to bed."

"Well, you know what we bought from Sid and Annie," she said. "Smoke sausage and cheese and crackers. But it's here whenever you want to eat."

"Now's as good a time as any."

"I think so, too. That's why I put the food out, over there on my bedroll."

Stepping over to the outspread bedroll, they sat down on the edge of the blankets and began eating. They ate in silence, both hungry after their long day's ride, for at noon they'd only nibbled a few bites of food while in the saddle. At last Ki stood up and brushed the cracker crumbs from his trousers.

"It's not quite dark yet," he observed, "but I want to sleep now. I'll set my mind to wake me up in about two hours and work on my horse's leg again."

Monica looked at him, here eyes open wide in astonishment. "Do you mean you can wake up any time you want to, even after an exhausting day like this one's been?"

"Of course. Training the mind as well as the muscles is part of the teaching given in every *dojo*."

"And what's a *dojo?*"

"A school, Monica. A school where masters of their art teach combat without the use of weapons."

"Since the first time I saw you, Ki, I've wondered why you never wear a gunbelt. Every man you see in this part of the country does. And I would've felt—well, almost afraid to start looking for Jessie if I hadn't brought along that old rifle of my father's. Didn't they even teach you to use a gun at that *dojo* school you went to?"

Ki shook his head. "No. But I learned to use other weapons that are effective at a distance."

"I think I'd rather have a good rifle," Monica said.

"Even though I learned to use guns when I began my work with Alex Starbuck, I still preferred my own silent weapons," Ki told her. "Alex Starbuck was the target of many enemies for a number of years."

"That's what Jessie mentioned, but I saw she didn't want to talk about her father, so I didn't ask any questions."

"It is a very long story, but when you and Jessie become closer friends, I'm sure she will tell you more about Alex," Ki said. He stepped over to his bedroll and went on, "I won't disturb you when I get up to go tend the horse. Moving noiselessly is something else I learned in the *dojo*."

As Blake Laird guided Jessie through the darkness, she formed a mental picture of the Mountie's camp, and began looking for a tent and campfire among the pines. Since he'd told her the camp was only a ten-minute hike away, she kept peering ahead, trying to spot the glowing coals of

157

a campfire that would pinpoint its location. She made no effort to conceal her surprise when Laird stopped and turned to her in a small clearing where a sheer rock wall towered at the back of a pocket of vegetation.

"Here we are," he said. "I'll go ahead and light the Primus so it'll be easier for you to find your way."

"I—I don't understand," Jessie stammered. "I don't see any sign of a camp here, and I'm sure I would, even as dark as it is here."

"Good," Laird nodded. "I take that as a compliment, Miss Starbuck. Please stay where you are. I won't be half a mo'."

Jessie followed the Mountie's shadowy form with her eyes as he took a half-dozen steps to the stone barrier that rose at the back of the little dell. Suddenly his shadowy form vanished. Jessie was still blinking to make sure her eyes weren't deceiving her when light flared from the face of the cliff for a moment. It faded quickly into a steady vee-shaped glow that would have been invisible a dozen paces away. The glow was blotted out by a shadow, and Laird appeared out of the gloom to stand in front of the cliff, outlined against its face by the faint light that came from a high triangular fissure which split its stone face.

"Welcome to my camp, Miss Starbuck," he said. "Won't you step inside and have a cup of tea?"

"Is this your camp?" she asked as she stepped across to the Mountie. "I was looking for a tent or shelter of some kind."

"I'm afraid I can't offer you a tent," he replied. "If I hadn't stumbled on this crack in the rock, I'd've found a hollow stump or a patch of brush. You see, Miss Starbuck, tents don't grow in the forest like trees, and they can be seen from quite a distance."

"Of course." Jessie nodded. "I've had to hide a few times myself, and when I do, I look for a natural place that no one will notice."

"Very shrewd," Laird agreed. "If you're trying to avoid

being seen by a bunch of murdering outlaws, you don't let them know where you're sleeping, or there might be a morning when you wouldn't wake up because they'd seen your camp during the day."

As Laird spoke, Jessie was surveying the cleft. It ran back in a vee for a dozen feet into the high stone formation. A huddle of blankets lay just inside the opening on the thick covering of windblown pine needles spread over its floor. At the rear of the vee a small Primus stove that looked like a thin taper in a teacup burned with a flame no larger or brighter than a candle. A rifle and a knapsack leaned against one wall beside the teacup-sized stove.

"I'm afraid it's rather bare," Laird apologized. "But it's home until I have Ventner and his men safely in irons. Now I'll see what I can fix up in the way of sleeping accomodations, if you don't mind sharing my crowded quarters."

"I'm sure I'll sleep more comfortably here than in Dutch Ventner's cabin," Jessie replied. "But we haven't talked about what we're going to do tomorrow."

"Let's rest first, Miss Starbuck," Laird said. "We'll be able to think more clearly when we wake up."

"I won't object to some sleep," Jessie told the Mountie. "But I don't want to wake up and find that you've gone off to try to capture those three men by yourself."

"You have my word that I won't leave until after we've had our talk," Laird promised. "Now let me arrange a blanket for you in the crevice here. Just to be safe, I'll sleep outside tonight in case Ventner and his men start prowling before daybreak."

As Ki had told Monica he would, he woke after two hours of sleep and sat up in his bedroll just as though someone had called to him. His pupils were dilated from sleep, and as soon as Ki opened his eyes he had his night-vision. The little vale where he and Monica had stopped was totally still. The moon was in its dark phase, but the brilliant stars of the high Western country shed enough light for him to see quite clearly.

Monica lay motionless, sleeping soundly, her head resting on one forearm, her blankets pulled high over her shoulders against the cool night breeze. The night was so still that he could hear the soft sibilance of her steady breathing. At the edge of the bushes, her tethered horse was swaying gently in its own light slumber. A few yards from shore, Ki's mount stood in the river's shallow. It was awake, but as he walked toward the water's edge Ki could see that it was now standing on all four hooves, not favoring the one it had strained.

He waded out to the horse through the knee-keep water and lifted its injured hoof. The dark, smooth surface of the slow-flowing river reflected the myriad of stars, and amplified their light. Ki looked at the horse's injured pastern-joint and saw that the swelling had diminished now to a small puffiness. He began squeezing and rubbing the swollen joint, the horse stirring and whinnying occasionally as Ki manipulated the sprain.

When he'd done all that he thought was possible to speed the healing process, Ki waded back to shore and started for his blankets. His wet trousers clung to his shins as he walked, and he stopped beside his bedroll to try to wring them dry. No matter how hard he twisted and squeezed, the trouser legs still seemed clammy. He looked at Monica, a shadowy form under her blankets, and decided to slip out of the trousers and let them dry in the night air. Taking them off, he spread them on the grass within easy reach, and stepped over to his bedroll.

"You've answered a question that I've been puzzling over ever since you started down to the river, Ki," Monica said suddenly.

When Ki looked at her he saw that she was sitting up in her bedroll. She'd taken off her blouse, and the tips of her swelling breasts were dark against her ivory skin.

Monica went on, "I've been trying to think of a subtle

160

way to persuade you to take your trousers off, and now I won't have to. Come to bed with me, Ki."

"I thought you were asleep!" Ki exclaimed.

"No. I've been lying here thinking about what I've missed these past few years, and calling myself a fool for not taking advantage of a time and place to enjoy being in bed with a man who appeals to me."

"And I appeal to you?" Ki asked as he walked slowly over to Monica's bedroll. "Why?"

"That's the first question I asked myself when I woke up from a dream that you and I were in bed together. I don't know the answer, Ki. I just know that I want you here with me, as naked as I am, feeling you inside me."

Ki realized that he would be less than human if he failed to respond to Monica's honest invitation, but there was more in his thoughts than that. He was recalling the appeal he'd squelched earlier when he'd been stirred by the subtle aroma of her body that had reached him while he was clasping her to him during the last moments of their ride. Remembering as he looked at her generous breasts and smooth shoulders, Ki felt himself stirring. He shed his jacket and slid his loincloth down his sturdy legs without unwrapping its folds.

Monica gasped when she saw his beginning erection. "Hurry, Ki!" she urged. "I've been lying here waiting and wondering, and now I don't want to wait any longer!"

Ki slipped into the bedroll beside Monica and took her in his arms. She cried out when he went into her; she clasped her thighs around him and rose to meet his lusty strokes. Then the night closed in around them and shut them into the private domain of lovers who were finding a fresh world in one another.

Chapter 15

When the tiny scraping noise aroused Jessie from her sound sleep she awoke, instantly alert. The light in the crevasse was only a bit brighter than it had been when she'd dropped off to sleep, but now it had the grayish tinge that warned of first dawn and the impending sunrise. Through habit she'd taken off her gunbelt and laid it beside her before crawling into the makeshift bed Blake Laird had fixed for her the night before. Jessie reached for the gunbelt with a swiftness that had become almost instinctive after years of living with danger just around the corner.

Not until her hand touched the empty holster and found no gun-butt to grasp did she remember that Ventner had taken the Colt away from her when he'd captured her. Then the other events of the previous day returned with a rush of memory, and she sat up. Looking toward the opening of the rock-cleft she saw the Mountie standing in the tapering vee, his broad shoulders shutting out most of the gray dawn light that showed beyond him in the brightening sky.

"I hoped I could come in and get my Primus without disturbing you, Miss Starbuck," he said. "I forgot to take it outside with me last night, and thought you'd like a cup of coffee when you woke up."

"It's time for me to wake up anyhow, I'm sure," Jessie replied. As she threw the blanket aside and stood up, she went on, "And as a favor, would you please be a bit less formal? I'd really prefer it if you'd call me Jessie."

"Whatever you wish, of course." Laird nodded. "My superiors wouldn't approve, of course, but out here in the field, regulations made up by office types aren't always practical. Jessie it shall be. And Blake, please; at least as long as we're not with one of my officers."

"I certainly wouldn't want to cause you any trouble." Jessie smiled. "I'll try to remember. And yes, I would like coffee."

"As late as it is, it's early for the men we're after—or who're very probably out looking for you right now," Laird went on. "Suppose we move camp first, and have coffee and a bite of breakfast after we're in a less exposed place?"

"Whatever you say. I'm ready to move now if you are. Those outlaws are probably out and around by now, looking for me. I'd hate for them to catch us off guard."

"If they're out, they haven't gotten close to us," Laird told her. "I'd have heard them if they had. They're so used to being the only ones around their hideout that they don't even try to move quietly. But you're right; the outlaws will be on the prowl soon, even if they aren't already, and we'll have to move to a better place at once."

"Do you have someplace in mind?"

"As a matter of fact I do. It'll mean a little wading to hide our tracks, but I'm pretty sure they won't find us."

"I'll be ready to go as soon as I get my boots on," Jessie said. Then she added, "Does this mean you've changed your plans to include me?"

"I did a lot of thinking before I went to sleep last night, but let's put off talking about plans until we've moved. I'll put the loose gear into my pack and we'll get started."

Jessie watched the Mountie as he stuffed the Primus stove and a small stew-pot into his pack, added the box of rifle shells that had been lying on the floor of the crevasse, and began rolling up the blanket that had been her bed.

"Are we moving out of here completely?" she asked.

"There's no way to be sure," he answered. "After a lot of cases I've learned that no two situations are exactly alike and that things seldom happen twice in the same way."

"So you don't like to make plans?"

"That's not what I said," Laird reminded her. "Of course I make plans. We're going to make some plans as soon as we get to a better place to wait. But I don't make plans and freeze them in my mind. I always try to leave maneuvering room."

By now Jessie had smoothed her sleep-touseled hair and pushed her feet into her boots.

"I'm ready to go whenever you are," she said.

Laird shouldered the pack and picked up the rifle, then handed the weapon to Jessie.

"You'd better take this," he said. "There's no way of knowing where Ventner and his men are now. I've got my pistol, if we happen to run into them."

"Are you making me your deputy?" Jessie asked.

"We're not authorized to deputize anybody in the Mounted," he said. "But you certainly have the right to protect yourself if we happen to run into trouble. Now let's move along. We don't have very far to go, but there's no use staying here. It's a bit too close to Ventner's hideout for comfort."

Jessie followed Laird as he circled behind the split rock-face and started following the course of the creek. The thick forest kept them close to the edge of the bank as Laird led the way, setting their pace at a fast walk, moving with the certainty of a man who knows exactly what his destination is. They'd walked only a quarter of an hour when he stopped and motioned for Jessie to come up beside him.

"Is this the place?" Jessie asked, looking around. "All I see is that big, bare boulder that sticks out into the water. It's solid rock, you can tell that at a glance. And I don't see anything else except a bunch of scattered trees growing too far apart to provide any kind of cover."

"Just follow me," the Mountie said.

Laird started down the steep-sloping bank toward the creek. Jessie expected him to stop at the water's edge, but he did not. Without slackening his pace he waded toward the boulder. Then suddenly he vanished.

Jessie looked at the huge stone formation more closely than she had a moment earlier, but saw no fissure or crack into which her companion could have gone. She was still standing there trying to solve the mystery of Laird's disappearance when she heard his voice. It was strangely distorted, muffled, as though he was speaking in a small cellar.

"Hurry, Jessie!" Laird called. "You have to follow my footprints, and you won't be able to see them in a few minutes!"

Jessie half-ran, half-slid down the steep slope to the water's edge. The water of the creek lapped her boot toes when she stopped. She looked at the creekbed and saw the prints of the Mountie's boots. The current had already blurred their outlines, and Jessie took a deep breath and stepped into the water, then ran as she'd seen Laird do, toward the boulder.

She was within a yard of it before she saw the opening, a wide gap beneath the huge stone monolith and the water's surface. She started running toward it. The gap between stone and water seemed to grow as she got closer, and she needed only to duck her head as she went under the massive granite stone.

166

Under the jutting overhand of the massive boulder, there was plenty of light, even though it was a bit subdued. Laird stood on the level bank a yard or less from the gap where Jessie had entered. He was watching her approach, a wide smile on his rugged face. Jessie looked up and returned his smile as she stepped out of the inch-deep water and joined him.

"You certainly do find the most interesting hiding places I've ever seen, Blake," Jessie remarked, looking around them.

A few paces from their feet the little creek that ran past Ventner's hideout before it flowed into the river coursed over a submerged sandbank. The footprints Jessie and Laird had left as they splashed across the inch-deep sandbar to the shelter of the rock overhang that concealed them were already being washed away by the current. From above, on the bank of the creek, Jessie had not had a hint of the undercut bank below the huge stone monolith, where she and the Mountie now stood.

"I stumbled onto this place quite by accident," Laird told her. "When I picked up rumors that Ventner's hideout was on this creek, I was walking upstream looking for it when I saw an otter coming out of what I'd taken to be a solid rock formation. That got my curiosity aroused, and when I investigated and found the rock to be an overhang, I marked it in my mind as a possible shelter while I watched for Ventner to return. But a few days later I found the place we stayed last night and used it instead, because it's closer to Ventner's retreat."

"You don't suppose the outlaws know about this place, too?" Jessie asked as she looked back into the dim cavernous opening behind them.

"I doubt it. From what I've seen they stay close to their shanty. They're not interested in exploring the woods."

Jessie nodded. "It's much less exposed than the place you've been using. And I suppose we've come here to stay until dark? You do plan for us to try to capture Ventner and his men tonight, as I suggested?"

Laird nodded. "I've thought of it from all angles, Jessie. Even though our regulations are strictly against it, I'm going to depend on you just as I would another member of the force."

"We'll make a good team, I'm sure," Jessie said. "Now, let's get coffee started and have breakfast. We can make our plans while we eat."

When Monica stirred beside him, Ki woke at once and looked at her. Monica's face was still smooth in sleep, a tiny smile playing on her lips as though she was enjoying a pleasant dream. Ki wondered if she was, and if so, whether he figured in it. Then he slid lithely out of the bedroll and glanced around.

Although the sun had not yet come up, the sky was bright with the soft, gray dawn light that heralded the sunrise. Monica's horse stamped at the edge of the thicket where it was tethered, and Ki's mount was still standing quietly, knee-keep in the river.

Ki picked up his clothing, which was lying beside the blankets where he'd dropped the garments the night before. Stepping into his loincloth, then his trousers, he bent down to get his jacket and saw that Monica's eyes had opened since he first glanced at her. She was gazing up at him, smiling contentedly.

"You should've woken me up, Ki," she said. Then she shook her head, her smile broadening, and went on, "No. I guess it's just as well that you didn't. If you had, we'd both still be in these blankets."

"There's nothing I'd have liked better," Ki assured her. "But we've got a long day ahead, and every minute of daylight's important. I'm going to wade out and bring my horse in now. With any luck, his leg will be all right again, and we can get started as soon as we've had a bite of breakfast."

She nodded. "Go ahead. To save time later, I'll start putting things in our saddlebags and rolling up the blankets."

Ki sloshed through the chilly water of the river to his horse. Its pastern-joint looked normal when he lifted its leg out of the water, and as he waded to shore, leading the horse behind him, it showed no signs of limping. He tethered the animal near Monica's and joined her.

"Your horse seemed to be moving all right when I glanced at you coming out of the water," she said.

"I think it is. We'll soon find out. I hope its leg's in good shape, because today we won't be able to ride as close together as we did yesterday."

Monica was sitting beside her blankets. Ki's were rolled neatly, ready to be tied to his saddle strings. She'd smoothed out the blankets that had been her bed and placed the sack of food on them. She'd gotten dressed while Ki was at the river, and she looked at him now, her head cocked inquiringly, the beginning of a frown wrinkling her brow.

"Why not?" she asked.

Ki had just bitten off a piece of cheese and was nibbling at a cracker. He chewed and swallowed before he answered her.

"Because unless we spread out to cover more territory, we might miss finding Ventner's trail."

She frowned. "I got the idea that his hideout was right along the riverbanks."

Ki nodded. "So did I, from what Sid said. But we don't have any idea how close to the bank it is. We've got a lot of thick forest to search, Monica."

Monica had started eating now, and Ki waited patiently while she finished her mouthful.

"Yes," she said. "I know we're looking for a needle in a haystack, Ki. But surely he'd have this place of his close to the river—right on its bank, I'd imagine."

"That's my feeling, too. But Ventner's as cagy an out-

169

law as you're likely to find. He'd know that travellers use the river as a guide, and follow its banks, so he'd probably have his hideout somewhere away from the stream, not right at the water's edge."

"I hadn't thought of that." Monica frowned. "Maybe we shouldn't have started all by ourselves, Ki. We'd need a fifty-man posse to search the forest any distance from the bank."

"Getting together a posse in a town where nobody lives but thieves, crooks, and killers might present some problems," he pointed out. "A lawman usually calls a posse together and swears its men in as deputies."

"Without being sworn in, I suppose we're outlaws, too," Monica said thoughtfully. Then she smiled and went on, "If you can have such a thing as an outlaw posse, I guess we're it."

Ki nodded. "We probably are. And posses are supposed to ride. We'd better get started, because we've got a lot of country to cover before dark. Now that we've reached the river, we'll have to change our pattern. One of us should ride right along the edge of the stream, the other a half-mile or so away from the bank."

"You're thinking that Ventner might not have been heading for the river?" She frowned. "That we might not be able to pick up his trail just by following the bank?"

"Something like that," Ki said, and nodded. "If his hideout isn't right along the riverbank, he could've turned off before he got to the stream. If we just keep following the shoreline, we could miss his trail without knowing we'd been close to it."

"That hadn't occurred to me, but you're right," Monica agreed. "Do you want to follow along the bank, or shall I?"

"Whichever you prefer," Ki told her. "As long as the two of us cover as much ground as we can."

Monica was thoughtfully silent for a moment. Then she said, "Suppose I ride along the bank, then, Ki. The ground's likely to be softer close to the water, and tracks there would be easier to see."

"Then I'll cut away from the river about two miles and try to keep on a course parallel with it," Ki said. He frowned thoughtfully and went on, "This is one time when I'm a bit sorry that I don't carry a gun. It'd be nice if we could signal with a shot if we needed help or something. But if I hear you shooting, I'll get to you as fast as I can."

"I won't shoot unless there's a real reason, Ki," Monica promised. "If I do need help, or if I find a trail that might lead us to Ventner's hideout, I'll just angle toward you until I catch up. Shots would alert Ventner and his men, if we're close to their hideout."

Ki nodded. "Good. If I find anything promising, I'll ride toward you. Now, I'll saddle the horses while you roll up your blankets and we'll get started."

Less than a quarter of an hour later, what Monica had jokingly dubbed the "outlaw posse" was on the move.

"There's really not a great deal of planning to be done," Laird told Jessie as they sat on the yielding sand under the giant granite outcrop. "We'll start in time to get to their shanty just after dark. I've been watching the two men Ventner left there, and they're fairly well set in their habits. They eat supper right at dusk and then go to bed."

"Do you think Ventner being there will change things?" Jessie asked. "They'll probably be looking for me all day. Will that cause them to change their habits?"

Laird nodded. "I've thought of that possibility. They may go to bed a little later, but I'm sure that's the only change they'll make."

"I'd like to know a little more about the layout of their shack," Jessie said. "I never did get a really good look at the place. They took me inside almost the minute I got there. I know there's a stable behind the shack where they sleep, but that's about all."

"You know just as much as there is to know about the

171

place, then," Laird told her. "The ground behind the shanty and the stable rises very sharply. My guess is that they'll make a beeline for the river after they can't get to their horses."

"Why can't they? As I remember, the stable and shack are so close together that they're practically one building."

"Your memory's very good. They are one building, or rather the side of the shanty is one wall of the stable. But that's where you're going to be with my Webley. You can take cover behind the corner of the shack, and if any of them starts for the horses, don't be afraid to pull the trigger. I hope the idea that you might kill one of them doesn't bother you. Or does it?"

"I've shot at men before, Blake," Jessie replied dryly. "And hit most of them. I've never really enjoyed doing it, but all of the men I've shot have been criminals, some of them worse than Ventner."

"You didn't mention that before," Laird said. "It's something of a surprise, but I'm glad to hear it."

"Then go ahead with your plan," Jessie told him. "Where are you going to be? I don't want to hit you, shooting in the dark."

"You needn't worry. As soon as you're in place, I'll start for the shack. But I'll come up to the place from where I've been hiding, and I'll be running up from your right side. The outlaws will be coming from your left."

Jessie nodded. "That's good. There's not much of a way for me to mistake you for Ventner or one of his men."

"A very small chance." Laird nodded.

"Do you plan to take them dead, or alive?"

Laird did not reply for a moment. Then he said soberly, "We have a regulation in the Mounted Police, Jessie. We are not allowed to shoot at a suspected criminal unless he fires one or more shots at us, after we've identified ourselves as officers and demanded that he surrender peacefully."

"I don't think you'll have to worry about that tonight," Jessie said thoughtfully.

"Neither do I. Now, let's have that breakfast we've put off for such a long time," the Mountie said. "Then I'll spread the blankets and we'll rest until it's time to go. We've got a very busy night ahead of us!"

Chapter 16

Ki reined his horse to a halt and leaned forward in his saddle to get a better look at the pattern of hoofprints on the ground. After studying them for a moment he dismounted to look at them more closely. He followed the trail of overlapping, crescent-shaped marks for a dozen yards in each direction from the point where he'd stopped his horse, then mounted and turned the animal toward the river, drumming his heels into the horse's flanks to urge it to greater speed.

He'd covered the better part of two miles before he caught sight of Monica. She was riding along the riverbank, her horse moving at a walk. Ki shouted, but the distance was too great for his voice to carry. He drove his heels into the horse's sides and the tiring animal responded with a burst of speed.

Before Ki had covered half the distance between him and Monica, she saw him and waved. Ki reined in, stood up in his stirrups and gestured for her to join him. Monica

175

understood the signal at once, turned her horse, and rode toward him. Knowing that they might still have a long ride ahead, Ki did not go to meet her, but waited until she reined in beside him.

"Did you find their trail?" she asked eagerly.

"I'm sure I did," he said, nodding. "There's a pretty well-beaten path north, maybe a dozen or more sets of hoofprints. Two sets were a lot sharper than the others. They're really sharp and fresh. They could only have been left by Jessie and Ventner on the way to his hideout."

"If we're going to find them in time to help Jessie, we'd better hurry, then," Monica said.

Ki was looking upward, his eyes slitted as he gauged the position of the sun. Blinking, he turned back to look at Monica. Her face was sober, her eyes showing her concern.

"We don't have any time to waste," he agreed. "We've only got about two more hours of daylight. Even if we've finally found the trail, we don't know how much farther we have to go, or even exactly where those prints are going to take us."

Ki turned his horse and with Monica riding beside him, started back toward the trail that it had taken them so many hours to unearth.

Jessie woke with a start and gazed around the hidden grotto below the big granite ledge. Their hideout was darker; the gleam that had crept up through the water of the creek was no longer bright with filtered sunlight, but fading into gray.

Blake Laird was still sleeping. Jessie studied his relaxed features in the fading light. This was the first time she'd seen him totally relaxed. Since their first encounter the Mountie had always been on his feet and alert. With his face smoothed in sleep, the crow's feet at the corners of his eyes smoothed out, as did the lines from his nose to the edges of his lips, and he looked much younger than he did awake.

176

Some sixth sense must have told Laird that he was being watched, for he opened his eyes and looked up at Jessie. At first his face did not change. Then he leaned up on one elbow and spoke, and with his movement the youthful look of sleep faded and he was once again the ruggedly mature man she'd seen at their first encounter. Jessie found it hard to realize that that they'd met only a few hours ago.

"I'm as hungry as a bear," Laird said as he sat up and looked around. "And I'd imagine you must be, too."

"A bit," Jessie admitted. "But I just woke up myself."

"I'm afraid my rations are running a bit short," Laird told her as he got to his feet and went to his haversack. "I didn't count on spending so much time having to wait for Ventner to show up at his hideout, and I didn't realize that I'd have such a charming guest."

"I'm sure we'll manage," Jessie said. "And if your plans work out, this will all be over tonight."

"They'll work," Laird said confidently. He rose to his feet in one lithe move and stepped over to his haversack. After rummaging in it for a moment, he turned back to Jessie and said, "I'm afraid we'll have to settle for dried apples and bannock. That seems to be all that I have left."

"I hope you're not short of coffee. I think I'd enjoy almost anything if there's a good hot cup to go with our meal."

"Coffee is something I always have," the Mountie told her. "And I'll light the Primus now, so it'll be ready by the time we've finished eating. Then we'll run over our plans again, and by then it'll be time for us to start up the creek for Ventner's hideout. I'd like to get into position before the light's gone. Then we'll both be sure of what our targets are."

Ki reined in, and as Monica reached his side he turned to her and said, "I think we'd better stop and leave the horses here while I scout ahead on foot. Since we turned off along this creek and started through this wooded country a little while ago, these tracks we've been following are a lot harder to see, especially now that the light's failing."

"Whatever you say, Ki," Monica nodded. "You've had a lot more experience at things like this than I have."

Ki pointed ahead to the huge rock formation that jutted out into the creekbed and went on, "That'll be a good place for you to wait for me. I have a very strong hunch that we might find Ventner's hideout upstream along this creek. He'd want to be close to a water supply, and he'd want to be away from the main trail along the river, too."

Reining in beside the huge chunk of granite, they dismounted. Ki studied the ground around the big rock formation for a moment and said, "Somebody's been around here lately, but there's such a thick layer of pine needles on the ground that I can't tell much about the footprints; the tracks are too confused. I'll tether the horses and scout up along the creek, Monica. I won't be gone very long."

"You're not going to get too close to Ventner's hideout if you find it, are you?" she asked. "I'd hate to think—"

"Don't worry," Ki broke in. "I'll be back in just a few minutes. All I intend to do is find out whether we're still on the right trail, or whether we've lost it." He finished looping the horses' reins around the trunk of a small pine and took Monica's rifle out of its saddle scabbard. He walked back to her and handed her the weapon.

"There's not much chance that you'll be disturbed," he said. "But for all we know, we might be too close to Ventner's hideout for comfort. You'd better keep this with you, just in case."

"All right, Ki." She nodded. "Be careful, now."

Ki nodded, then, frowning as he studied the scuffed footprints, their outlines vague and indecipherable in the deep layer of duff that covered the ground, he started along the edge of the creekbed.

Left to herself, Monica walked idly along the edge of the granite overhang, looking around at the thick pine forest and at the chuckling waters of the creek as they danced over its sandy bed. A scraping noise drew her attention back to the overhang. She turned in time to see a man's head rising above the edge of the huge rock overhang.

Swinging her rifle, not stopping to aim, Monica triggered off a shot. The slug was wide. It grated with a muffled screech against the surface of the granite, only inches from the man's head, raising a spurt of powdered rock and chips that flew into his face. With a muffled groan, he dropped below the edge of the outcrop and vanished.

Monica began running toward the rim of the shelving granite, levering a fresh round into the rifle's chamber as she moved. She reached the end of the big rock and looked down, saw the man lying on the sandy creek-bank, his hands covering his face. She swung her rifle around for a second shot.

Before her finger tightened on the trigger she saw movement beneath her at the edge of the granite formation. She shifted her aim to cover what she was sure was a fresh threat. Her finger was closing on the trigger, but she stopped its pressure just in time when Jessie appeared as if from nowhere. Jessie wasted no time on the man lying at her feet, but looked up, shouldering the rifle she carried.

"No, Monica!" Jessie cried when she saw her friend bringing up her weapon. "Don't!"

Monica lowered the rifle, her mouth wide with surprise. "Jessie!" she exclaimed. "What—"

"There's no time to talk!" Jessie snapped. She dropped her rifle on the creek-bank and hurried toward the man lying at the water's edge. "Come down here and help me with Blake!"

Smothering the question that rose to her lips, Monica ran along the edge of the granite shelf to join Jessie, who'd now reached the recumbent man and was dropping to her knees on the ground beside him.

"Move your hands away, Blake," she said. Then, as Monica reached her side, she turned and said, "Help me hold his head steady and don't let him rub his eyes."

Looking down at the Mountie again, she went on, "Keep your head still, Blake, and open your eyes as wide as you can."

Laird's eyelids twitched, but he seemed unable to get his eyes open. With Monica helping her to hold the Mountie's head cradled on her lap, Jessie carefully pulled up one eyelid. The pupil of the eye was not bleeding, but it was powdered with granite dust. Letting the lid slide gently down, Jessie looked at his other eye and found it in the same condition.

"I don't think it's bad," Jessie told him. "Just a lot of granite dust. Can you see me?"

"I can't see anything but a blur," Laird replied.

"Hold still, now," Jessie went on. "I'm going to wash your eyes and get rid of the dust." Turning to Monica, she said quickly, "Help me hold his eyelids open, Monica. You hold one eye, I'll hold the other. I need one hand free to trickle water into them."

Moving slowly and carefully, Jessie cupped her hand and lowered it into the clear water flowing close beside her. She lifted the hand and let a small stream trickle into one of the Mountie's eyes. The water flowed over his exposed eyeball and trickled down his temple, carrying most of the granite specks with it. Moving her hand with equal care, Jessie treated the other eye in the same fashion, then repeated the process.

"Just let your eyes close naturally now," she said. "And tell me if you feel any specks in them."

Blake blinked his eyes, wincing as their lids moved, then said, "They still feel like somebody's been rubbing them with sandpaper, though."

Jessie nodded. "I'll wash them again. Lie still."

Dipping her cupped hand in the water, Jessie trickled more of it into one eye, then the other. Blake blinked several times, slowly and cautiously at first, then faster.

"I can see pretty clearly now, but my eyes still feel sore," he told Jessie. "It'll probably take a little time for

180

them to clear up completely."

"Oh, I'm so sorry!" Monica exclaimed. "I didn't know who you were, or I never would've shot!"

"I might've pulled the trigger, too, if I'd been in your place. And I'm just grateful that you missed," Blake told her. He sat up, still blinking and shaking his head, and added, "I'm sure I'm all right now."

Jessie said, "If you still don't feel comfortable, I'll—" She broke off and reached for the rifle she'd dropped when she hurried to attend to the Mountie. "There's somebody coming," she went on. "We'd better—" She stopped short when Ki appeared, dodging through the trees beside the creek. "Ki! You don't know how glad I am to see you!"

"No more than I am to see you," Ki told her. "And just about as surprised, I'm sure."

"I managed to get away from Ventner last night," Jessie said. "Luckily, I ran into Blake, here." Breaking off, she turned to Blake and went on, "I've told you about Ki, and here he is. And this is Monica Ransom. I've mentioned her, too."

"I'm glad to see you both," the Mountie said. "But you especially, Ki. From what Jessie's told me, you'll be a valuable third man for our foray on Ventner's cabin tonight."

"You're not going to be able to shoot tonight, if there's any shooting done," Jessie told the Mountie. "Ki and I will carry out our plan."

"Now hold on!" Laird protested. "Neither of you is an officer of the law!"

"Does that matter, as long as we're fighting the lawless?" Ki asked. "Jessie and I are used to working together —fighting together, too."

"But it's not—"

"Blake," Jessie broke in, "you wouldn't even think of giving up our plan, and I'm sure you wouldn't want it to fail."

"Of course not, but—" Blake began.

"No buts," Jessie said. "With you and Monica backing us up, there's not as big a chance of failing as there'd be if you and I were alone. Please, don't be unreasonable."

"But I can't fail to do my duty!" Laird insisted. "If—" He stopped short, blinking, and brought a hand up to cover his eyes. He held his palm pressed against his face while the others stood silent, watching him.

"You see now, don't you?" Jessie asked. "It's going to take two or three days for you to get all those specks of rock out of your eyes. Suppose they failed you at a critical time while we were facing Ventner and his thugs tonight? Besides, it's not as though you were stepping aside for two strangers."

"All right," Laird said reluctantly. "I'll be your backup, and just so it'll be official, I'll make a formal arrest. That way, we'll be sure that Ventner and his gang get what's coming to them."

"It shouldn't be all that difficult to surprise them, Ki," Jessie whispered as they stood behind the largest tree in the pine forest that surrounded Ventner's hideout. "I can tell from the way they've slowed down in their talk that all three of them are getting sleepy."

"No wonder," Ki replied. "They seem to've covered a lot of ground today, looking for you in every place but the right one."

"I suppose they did what was logical for them," Jessie said. "They'd think I'd start back toward the town. I'm sure that's what they would've done."

For the past quarter of an hour, Jessie and Ki had been crouching in the concealment of a thick clump of seedling pines only thirty or forty yards from the cooking-fire where the outlaws were gathered. They'd heard most of the outlaws' conversation, which had been devoted chiefly to gripes about their lack of success in tracking Jessie down. It was obvious from their conversation that it had never

182

occurred to the thugs to concentrate their search closer to the shanty.

Ventner was hunkered down in front of the dying coals of the cooking-fire, which were quickly being reduced to ashes, while Bracer and Marty faced him across the fire pit. Only a few live flames flickered in the shallow pit, and it was obvious that even these would not last much longer. Before Ki had a chance to reply to Jessie's comment, Ventner stood up and stretched.

"Well, this ain't been a good day, and I'm about as mad as I am tired," he said. "If you two bastards had been doing your job right, one of you'd've been standing watch last night over that Starbuck woman, and she never would've got away."

"We'll pick up her trail for sure, tomorrow," Bracer said. "She's afoot, and it stands to reason she ain't going to move no faster'n our horses."

"Sure," Marty agreed. "We'll snag onto her tomorrow. She ain't had time enough to go very far."

"We'd better find her," Ventner growled. "She's the only witness that can testify against me for killing Bella, and I got to put her outta the way before she spills what she seen to some sheriff or judge. Now we all better turn in. We got a lot of ground left to cover, so I wanta get started soon as there's light enough to see by."

As the outlaws straggled into the shanty, Jessie whispered to Ki, "We'll give them time to get settled for the night. Then you slip in, and I'll stay by the corner of the shack to keep any of them from getting away, just as we've planned."

"I remember," Ki said. "And I'll do my best just to disable them, so that our Mounted Police friend will have some prisoners to take back with him. But I hope he understands that we didn't guarantee to deliver any."

"I'm sure he'll understand, whatever happens. But remember that I owe him a great ideal for taking care of me."

Patiently, Jessie and Ki stayed in position in the cover of the big pine while the minutes slipped away. At last Jessie said, "I don't think there's a chance that any of them will come out of the shanty again. We might as well start, Ki."

Moving with the smooth silence that they'd learned to use in their many fights against the cartel's hired killers, they started toward the shanty. As they drew closer they could hear the rumblings of the snores coming from the three outlaws, and Jessie reached forward to touch Ki's shoulder.

Ki nodded without turning, and when they reached the shanty he slipped inside with the silence that came from many years of *ninjitsu* training. Jessie stopped outside the door, holding her rifle poised. The first signal she had that Ki was busy inside was a yowl of pain. Then Marty's voice shattered the silence still further.

"Leggo, dammit!" he yowled. "Bracer! Ventner! Give me a hand! Some kinda spook's got me!"

A shot split the night, followed by another. Then Ventner ran out of the door. Jessie caught the glint of metal from the revolver in his hand. The outlaw bumped into Jessie, sending her sprawling on the ground. She held on to her rifle, and when she looked up and saw Ventner standing over her, leveling his pistol at her, Jessie swung the rifle's muzzle toward him and fired.

Ventner was knocked backward by the impact of the heavy rifle slug. His finger closed on the trigger of his pistol as he staggered into the shanty wall, but he no longer had control of the weapon. The revolver's slug thunked harmlessly into the ground inches away from Jessie's head while the dying outlaw slid slowly down the wall and collapsed on the ground.

Only silence was coming from the cabin now. Jessie was getting to her feet when Ki came out. He looked at Ventner's body, then at Jessie.

"You didn't have much choice, either, I see," he said.

"No. He had his pistol in his hand when he came out the door," she replied.

"I couldn't save a prisoner for the Mountie, either," Ki confessed. "While I was holding one of the outlaws in front of me in a tiger claw to put him to sleep, the other man shot him."

"He meant the bullet for you, I'm sure," Jessie said.

"Of course," Ki said, and nodded. "But when he fired that shot I knew he'd be likely to get me with his next one, so I killed him with a *shuriken*."

Jessie shook her head and said, "And Ventner's dead, too. So Blake Laird will be going home empty-handed."

"Not quite, perhaps, Jessie." Laird spoke through the darkness as he and Monica came up to the shanty. "From what you've told me about that town Ventner was trying to start as an outlaw retreat, I'm sure I'll find more than one criminal there who's on my list of wanted men."

"Then I suppose you and Ki will leave things to him, and start back to your ranch in Texas," Monica sighed. "I'm going to miss you."

Her eyes on Blake Laird, Jessie said slowly, "You know, Monica, Ki and I could use a few days of rest before we start. If you don't object to our company, we'll just stay here awhile."